First published in Great Britain in 2021 by
Michael O'Mara Books Limited
9 Lion Yard
Tremadoc Road
London SW4 7NQ

A CIP catalogue record for this book is available
from the British Library.

Papers used by Michael O'Mara Books Limited are natural,
recyclable products made from wood grown in sustainable forests.
The manufacturing processes conform to the environmental
regulations of the country of origin.

ISBN: 978-1-78929-303-6 in hardback print format
ISBN: 978-1-78929-304-3 in ebook format

1 2 3 4 5 6 7 8 9 10

www.mombooks.com

Designed by Ed Pickford
Page layout and typeset by Design 23

Printed and bound by CPI Group (UK) Ltd, Croydon, CR0 4YY

MIX
Paper from
responsible sources
FSC® C020471

A YEAR
IN THE LIFE OF
ANCIENT
GREECE

THE REAL LIVES OF THE
PEOPLE WHO LIVED THERE

PHILIP MATYSZAK

Michael O'Mara Books Limited

Contents

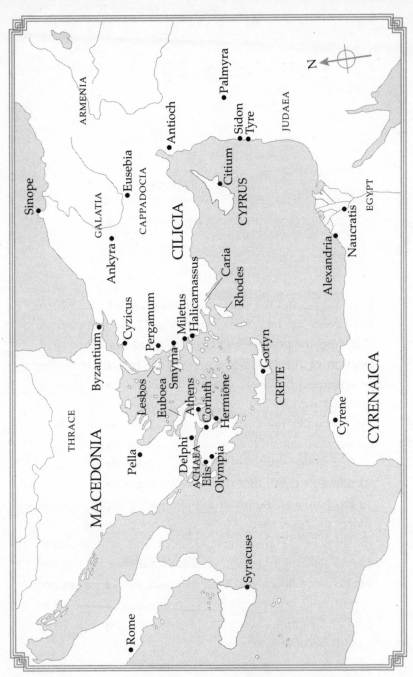

THE HELLENISTIC WORLD

Introduction

It is 248 BC, and the start of what is known to the people of Greece as the fourth year of the 132nd Olympiad. At this time, the peninsula of Greece represents only a small fraction of the Hellenistic world (the regions inhabited or colonized by Greek speakers) – one already enlarged by colonization but made immeasurably greater still by Alexander the Great, the Macedonian leader who, a century previously, had conquered the East as far as India.

Just over two generations have passed since Alexander's death, but now Greeks battle Indian armies on the banks of the Indus and Spanish irregulars on the shores of the western Mediterranean. Greeks live in the shadows of the pyramids in Egypt and in Alexander's city of Iskandar, which is now Kandahar in modern Afghanistan. It is a vast, strange world, full of danger and opportunity, but it is also a world in which taxes must be paid and routine chores completed every day. The exotic quickly becomes mundane.

Yet no matter how far they may be from their ancestral home, the Greeks abroad remain stubbornly Greek. They still worship their ancestral gods, exercise in their gymnasiums and come from near and (very) far to participate and compete in the already ancient rites of the Olympic Games.

In this book, we follow eight Greeks in very different situations, whose lives are in one way or another touched by the 133rd Olympiad. Though the people themselves are fictional, their lives are not. Each person has been described with the help of modern archaeological advances, which have progressed beyond a search for statues to place in museums to a science that now spends more time excavating dunghills than palaces.

And while palaces might yield golden treasures, there are greater prizes to be found in these dunghills and rubbish dumps, because in them we find traces of the real people of Greece. Not the kings and generals who feature in the histories of Thucydides and Polybius, but the ordinary men and women who paid the king's taxes and died in his armies. Given what archaeologists know of ancient architecture, they can make a fair reconstruction of what a building looked like from studying the foundations alone; we now know enough of the lives of ordinary Greeks to do the same sort of thing in the social sciences to recreate the lives of some ancient Greeks from the evidence of antiquity.

My aim in this book is to reconstruct the everyday lives of these ordinary people and what their world was like in the year 248 BC. At this time, the Greeks of Egypt were building the Great Library and Lighthouse of Alexandria, and elsewhere, science, philosophy and literature were advancing the standard of civilization. Though their occupation of Egypt, Syria and the Levant lasted but a moment in historical terms, to the Greeks of the time, their new, vast world seemed eternal and unchanging. This book reconstructs what it might have been like to live there.

A Note on Chronology

When Thucydides began to write his epic *The History of the Peloponnesian War*, he found he had a problem with time. Not that he did not have plenty of it, being an exile with nothing else to do, but he lacked the means to describe its passing.

In the modern West, this is straightforward. The years count from an exact date, which was originally (and inaccurately) believed to be when Christ was born. Each year starts on 1 January and, in every Western culture, months have a consistent number of days, with weekends arriving reliably on the sixth day of the week. Thursday, *Donnerstag* and *giovedì* are all the same day and happen at the same time of the same month.

Ancient Greece could not have been more different. Everyone's years started counting from a different date, be it from the founding of the city, a legendary event or the rule of a particularly distinguished individual. Years were named for individual leaders, such as kings or archons, and were different from city to city. Nor did the year start at the same time. Some states liked the idea of starting a year with the autumn equinox, while others started six months later in the spring. Some kicked the year off at the time of a particular religious festival (though no one seems to have chosen the bizarre and arbitrary time of some ten days after the winter solstice, since where would be the sense in that?).

Once the year had begun, whenever it began, the months were not only equally arbitrary but also flexible. If the city fathers decided that the civic calendar was a bit packed in one month, they might extend it by ten days or so, and steal days off other months to compensate. Since no sane landlord would rent a building on those terms, rents tended to be paid according to lunar months, so that in Athens alone there were competing calendars, including the lunar, the religious, the civic and the solar.

The Antikythera Mechanism

To make sense of all this and to date the year in this book, we have adopted the same solution as the Greeks. Imagine you are a merchant from Corinth who wants to buy silk from a dealer in Sardis in Asia Minor. To reconcile the different calendars of the participants in the deal, the merchant uses the world's first analogue computer.

By inputting the phase of the moon, the time of moonrise and the location of select constellations into the mechanism, the merchant uses it to determine the exact date in Corinth, wherever he might be in the known world.

This is then compared with the local calendar and, by advancing the input data to a future Corinthian date, the local date for delivery can be established. So too can the time of expected eclipses and similar phenomena, as well as the dates of great sporting events, such as the Olympic and Pythian Games.

We know the Greeks used such a mechanism because one was retrieved in 1901 from a shipwreck off the island of Antikythera, which lies between Greece and Crete. Since the mechanism was designed to make sense of the chronological anarchy of the Hellenistic era, it seems logical that in this book we should follow the system of the mechanism and resolve all dates to the Corinthian calendar.

By this calendar, our year starts with the autumn equinox, as did each year in the little Peloponnesian state of Elis where the Olympic Games were held. In colder northern climes, autumn sees the dying of the year, but in Greece autumn meant the end of the dry, hot and unproductive summer. It was when the first seasonal rains began to fall, signalling a new beginning.

Prologue

◒◒◒◒◒◒◒◒◒◒◒◒◒◒◒◒◒◒◒

The rain sluicing off the roof of the temple of Hera in Elis begins to slacken, and those sheltering beneath the portico prepare to leave and go their separate ways. An attendant of the temple watches them depart, regretfully aware that he will never know whether or not the assumptions he has made of this little group of strangers are correct.

That most are visitors to the city is clear enough but then, with the Olympics just ended, the city is packed with visitors to the Games who are now about to take their leave. A rangy young man paces restlessly between the columns of the portico – he has the build of a competitor, a runner probably – and the older man with him is almost certainly his trainer. But that's an easy deduction, as is the identification of the little family group in the corner. These are native Eleans, as shown by their dress and accent, with a shivering girl wrapped in her husband's cloak and a short, stout woman fussing around both with what can only be motherly concern.

But what to make of the stocky, balding man who, on his arrival, carefully examined the structure of the temple frontage and then spent the rest of the time glaring at the building as though it had personally offended him? Or the brown-haired girl with a horse tattoo on her neck who is solicitously attending that gaunt older man in the rich clothes – is she a slave, a lover or a nurse?

Then there is the dignified gentleman with the harsh Macedonian accent who had swept in from the rain with three servants and the athlete in tow, and ordered the attendant to bring him a chair as peremptorily as if he owned the temple. (The attendant has some experience of dealing with important dignitaries and had hastened to obey.) This man spends much of the rain-enforced delay talking quietly with a solitary woman who, despite being soaked through, has managed to keep mostly dry a leather case, which she carefully cradles in one arm. The woman has a confident air and striking good looks, but lacks the flirtatiousness of a courtesan – a professional musician, perhaps?

The attendant shakes his head as he surveys this mixed group of refugees from the storm. Where did they come from, and what peculiar combination of circumstance and chance brought them together beneath his temple's portico this wet afternoon? The attendant shrugs, for already the group are leaving, and he will never know.

Had the god within the temple granted omniscience to his attendant, this is what that man would have seen of their journey to this place, which began one year previously ...

ΦΟΙΝΙΚΑΙΟΣ ΑΡΧΕΣ

(October – Beginnings)

〰〰〰〰〰〰〰〰〰〰〰〰〰〰〰〰〰〰〰〰

The Farmer

On this clear autumn morning, Iphita is, as usual, up just before dawn. As a farmer in the small Peloponnesian state of Elis in southern Greece, Iphita pays little attention to how the local magistrates formally designate the months and years. After all, when a month can be extended at the whim of the city council, and even the neighbours in Arcadia can't follow the dating of Elean years, why should Iphita bother? Her calendar is the timeless march of the seasons, and the westward spin of the moon across the sky in all its different phases.

Right now, the constellation of the Pleiades is being slowly washed from the dawn sky by the strengthening light of day, for the stars are low on the horizon. The setting of the Pleiades marks the start of the agricultural year and Iphita, studying her scrolls by lamplight, has decisions to make about her winter crop. In Greece, not much grows in the dry, hot summer, so early autumn is when the farmers check their seed stock and prepare to take a gamble on what the winter weather will bring. If great Zeus and Demeter are kind, and the autumn rains are abundant, then a farmer might take a chance on emmer wheat or millet. But should the winter thereafter be dry, then the farmers who sowed less thirsty crops, such as barley, will be congratulating themselves on their foresight.

For Iphita, whose lands lie partly along the banks of the Alpheus river, rainfall can always be supplemented by judicious irrigation, so what concerns her now is not so much the rainfall over the coming winter but rather how things will stand in twelve months' time, when she expects the field that she is contemplating will carry a short-lived but extremely profitable crop – a huge crowd of human beings.

Whatever esoteric name the city council has given the year, Iphita knows that what really matters is that this is the final year of the 132nd Olympiad. In twelve months' time, the 133rd Olympic Games will be celebrated in the precinct that adjoins Iphita's farm, and for generations her family have become ever more wealthy from catering to the hordes of tourists who attend the Games. Consider, for example, the field that runs parallel to the south of the sacred site of Altis, over which Mount Kronos looms on the northern side. For the past two years, this field has given a plentiful yield of wheat, but Iphita knows that wheat absorbs from the soil the divine essence of Demeter, the goddess of the grain. When repeated sowings and

SOWING TIME IN GREECE

Each farmer's year was determined by the crop being grown and the land upon which it was sown. Few fields were rich enough to support two crops per year, and if a biannual crop was planned, the farmer would need to be sure of a good source of water to irrigate his fields through the long summer drought. Therefore most farmers started the year with the autumn rains. It was best to wait for the rains before sowing because breaking soil baked hard by the summer sun was brutal work given that most farmers worked with only the most basic tools. (Generally, the earth was broken rather than turned – deep ploughing only came with the Middle Ages.) Grain crops were generally harvested and processed in June and July, while olives, figs and other fruits were harvested in early autumn. Grapes were also harvested in autumn, so a farmer could at least be sure of a drink of fresh wine after a hard day preparing his fields.

harvests have exhausted that essence, the crops will fail. Usually Iphita would give this field a year to recover its energy, but next year, before the autumn sowing, some 300 tents will be on the field and, even more importantly, a hundred latrines. It's a source of quiet satisfaction to Iphita that not only do the unruly humans parked in her field thoroughly fertilize the ground before they depart, but they also actually pay her for doing the job.

Nevertheless, the field can't really support another wheat crop over the coming winter – fortunately, though, it won't have to. Iphita mentally begins to divide the field, working out which sections to allocate to which workers, and when her precious oxen will be available to turn the earth. Pulses – that's the thing. She'll sow the field with lentils, chickpeas and broad beans, each in separate beds and watered from the River Alphaeus should the rains be insufficient. As farmers have long known, Demeter's essence goes only into grain, and for this reason sowing pulses and legumes does not diminish the vitality of a field in the same way as wheat or barley would do.

If the local priest reports that the omens from her autumnal sacrifices are good, Iphita will tell her workers to start ploughing just after the next full moon, and to scatter the seed immediately following the next heavy rains. Three cycles of the moon should see the chickpeas and broad beans ripened, and if the season is cool the lentils will be harvested maybe ten days after that. Then, while the pulses are drying in baskets in the barn, she'll sow cucumbers, onions and garlic in the soil, which will have been refreshed by the pulses.

Usually, Iphita grows vegetables only for consumption by herself and her workers, for the rough roads of Elis make it too hard to get such perishable crops to market before they rot. But in an Olympic year, the market comes to Iphita and the stalls where she sells her crops are besieged by hungry attendees of the Games.

Yes, she has to move her livestock to the safety of adjoining farms, and yes, her workers have to prowl the orchards to keep out freebooting foragers (and amorous couples), and certainly the general hubbub and chaos will be unceasing for a fortnight. But when the crowds have ebbed away, and the broken pottery and other debris has been cleansed from the fields, the only sound in the shadow of Mount Kronos will be the clink of silver staters as Iphita fills her money bags and wonders how much of her bounty she can hide from the tax assessors.

Outside in the farmyard, there is a general stir and barking of dogs as the workers assemble for their morning instructions from Iphita's foreman. When her husband died, almost a decade ago now, most people had thought that this would be the end of the family farm. Iphita had given her husband just one child – a fat, lazy slob of a son – and no one had expected the young man to make a go of the brutally hard work of farming.

That son now lives in the city of Elis itself, and devotes his time to the lyre and the study of Epicurean philosophy. Nominally, he is the owner of the estate, but not for a moment would he dare gainsay the dictates of his formidable mother. Iphita is definitely in charge and has been since the early days, when she proved herself an unexpectedly capable student of her husband's techniques.

Now, together with her experienced foreman, she runs the farm with an iron hand. The son's only job – at which he has so far failed miserably – is to get married and produce some legitimate offspring to continue the family name. As she rises and pushes her scrolls aside, Iphita makes a mental note to have strong words with her son on that topic the next time they meet.

The Diplomat

Should they be powerful or influential enough, visitors to the court of the king of Macedon will inevitably find themselves seated on a couch and sipping an excellent wine (sourced locally from the Axios river valley) while Persaeus of Citium, the king's trusted advisor, carefully but politely assesses their potential usefulness. Persaeus is a stoic philosopher, an accomplished courtier and an eloquent advocate for his adopted land of Macedonia.

In Persaeus' opinion, few people have been misunderstood and unfairly treated more than the Macedonians. Consider, for instance, the southern Greeks. (To Persaeus, the Macedonians are the 'northern Greeks', and – like most Macedonians – bristles at any suggestion that Macedonians might be less Greek than, say, the Athenians.) The southern Greeks have spent their entire existence protected by the blood and sacrifice of the Macedonians, whose nation sits like a shield between the pampered folk of southern Greece and the wild hordes from the lands to the north.

At least once a generation, the Macedonians are called to arms to defend their mountain-girt kingdom from invaders from the lands beyond the Danube, often at the same time as their kingdom is simultaneously invaded from the east and west. And while Macedon has held off the barbarian hordes, how have the southern Greeks repaid that nation's sacrifices? By despising the Macedonians,

PTOLEMY II (284–246 BC)

After the death of Alexander the Great, one of his generals, a man called Ptolemy, headed for Egypt as quickly as he could. Ptolemy knew that Alexander's other generals would tear apart his empire in their struggle to rule it and Ptolemy wanted Egypt, which Alexander had captured in 332 BC. Ptolemy did not try to turn Egypt into a Macedonian state, but simply put himself at the top of the political and religious hierarchy by making himself pharaoh. Thereafter, Egypt consisted mostly of the very Greek city of Alexandria in the Nile delta, the occasional Greek settlement elsewhere in Egypt and the rest of the country, where life went on unchanged as it had for millennia.

Ptolemy fought several wars with the Seleucid kings who ruled the rump of Alexander's empire and tried hard to wrest control of Greece away from the Macedonians. When he died in 246 BC, there was a general sigh of relief across the Hellenistic world. Ptolemy's son was called Ptolemy after his father and 'Philadelphus' (loving brother) on account of his sister, whom he married. Ptolemy II developed Alexandria into a renowned centre of Greek culture all the while imitating his father by working tirelessly to subvert and undermine his fellow Hellenistic monarchs.

calling them half-breeds and semi-barbarians. 'Not even good enough to make decent slaves,' sneered one Athenian orator (shortly before the allegedly servile Macedonians subjugated Athens and brought the city under the yoke that it has resentfully borne ever since).

Consider the greatest of all the Greeks, all-conquering Alexander, the man who once and for all destroyed the Persian menace – a menace that had threatened Greek independence for generations. It was Alexander of Macedon who gave to Greece the Persian empire, an empire that stretches from the shores of the Mediterranean to the wastelands of the Gobi Desert.

You would think that breaking Persia would bring safety to Macedon and southern Greece, but no. After Alexander's death, his generals had inherited his conquests, and now Macedon is still at risk – but this time from those fellow Greeks who rule Alexander's former empire. Fortunately, the bulk of Alexander's conquests are currently held by an amiable king called Antiochus II of Seleucia. (Persaeus is one of the diplomats charged with ensuring that relations between the Seleucid king and Macedon remain cordial.)

The same cordiality cannot be extended to Ptolemy II, ruler of Egypt, another of Alexander's conquered kingdoms. Persaeus is a diplomat through and through and, in keeping with his stoic training, he endeavours to keep his voice calm and level whenever the topic of the very annoying Ptolemy comes up. When it does, however, even an untrained eye might note a slight empurpling of Persaeus' face and a whitening of the knuckles wrapped around his wine goblet.

To be frank, Ptolemy is a pain in the neck – though privately Persaeus tends to locate that pain somewhat further down. Macedon and Egypt have waged several lively little wars in the recent past and look as though they might wage a few more in the immediate future. The problem is Greece, which had been subject to the hegemony of Macedon ever since Alexander the Great took control of Greek affairs a century before. (Persaeus and other Macedonian courtiers wince politely should anyone be so uncouth as to describe Alexander's behaviour as 'conquest' – one does not conquer fellow Greeks.)

The advantage of Macedonian control of Greece is that the Greeks no longer stage the continual and tiresome little

PTOLEMY II, PORTRAYED HERE AS AN EGYPTIAN RULER

inter-city wars that were such a feature of earlier eras. The disadvantage of Macedonian control of Greece is that the Greek cities instead stage tiresome little rebellions against Macedon, and no sooner have the Athenians been slapped down for getting too uppity than up pop the Spartans, then the Arcadians, and so on, in a never-ending game of whack-a-hoplite.

Look at what's behind these little rebellions and the cause is immediately apparent – the agents of Ptolemy are everywhere in Greece, instigating disaffection with promises of diplomatic help, money, weapons and gold from Egypt's bottomless treasury. The people of southern Greece think of the years before they were subjugated by Macedon as a (largely illusory) golden age, and seem to think that, were Macedonian control to slip, then the era of Pericles, Socrates and Euripides would magically return.

Recently Ptolemy seduced the Athenians with promises of 'freedom' and incited the city into revolt. Then when the indignant Macedonians marched south to deal with the rebellion, Ptolemy promptly abandoned the Athenians whom he had so sedulously courted and left the city to its fate. With the Olympics approaching, Persaeus has no doubt that Ptolemy's agents will again be active, infiltrating the gathering to seek out disaffection, encourage division and dissent, and generally attempt to turn Greece into a hotbed of rebellion.

The only advantage that Persaeus can see in all this is that he might well have to go to the Olympics himself. If present in person, he can steer possible rebels back to the Macedonian fold with a bribe here, a subtle threat there and – should the worst come to the worst – perhaps a judicious assassination disguised as a freak javelin accident. Overall, a trip to the Olympics to nip potential problems in the bud could well turn out to be a well-spent excursion from home. And, there is the added bonus that the diplomat will have an excellent excuse for taking in all the splendour and spectacle of the Games.

The Slave Girl

Even before she leaves the house, Thratta knows that she can expect a beating on her return. Moodily, she sticks her tongue into the fleshy pouch between gum and lower lip where Athenians keep their small change. Small change in Athens is indeed small, and the two obols nesting against her teeth are the size of a grain of wheat. Coins this tiny are easily misplaced, and Thratta does not have enough of them to start with, so she will keep them securely in her mouth until she has to spit them carefully into some trader's saucer. She has done this many times before, but she offers prayers to gods whom she barely remembers that today will be the last time she goes on one of these difficult shopping trips.

Even if she goes to one of the more obscure markets near the Keremeikos, and even if she bargains desperately for wilted vegetables a week old, the slave girl knows that she will only just come back with enough food for the coming day's meals. Then her mistress will punish her for the inadequacy of the food, and then again for its poor quality.

It is not as if her mistress is not given enough house-keeping money by her husband. Thratta knows full well that her master budgets half a drachma a day for groceries and gives the money to his wife every ten days. In the women's quarters of the house, the part where the master seldom goes, there is a small vase filled with coin that Thratta's mistress has saved by skimping on household expenses just this year alone. Should the husband comment on the poor fare at dinner, however, it is Thratta who will suffer for the wife's parsimony. So now Thratta vows that, should the gods will it, today will be her last beating.

Unless, of course, this evening Thratta is beaten once more for the poor quality of her weaving. As do all female domestic slaves, Thratta spends a lot of time at the loom. She is expected to somehow produce the finest-quality garments, though all she can afford from her allowance are the cheapest fleeces – thin, burr-filled material matted with sheep's urine and excrement. Thratta was supposed to have turned this poor fabric to skeins of wool this morning before her mistress arbitrarily decided to send her shopping. Not that this shopping trip gets her out of weaving duties, so Thratta will be expected to work late into the night to make up her shortfall in wool production and doubtless will get punished in the morning for recklessly burning oil in the lamp. Sometimes Thratta thinks her mistress looks for excuses to whip her simply because the old κασσωρίς enjoys doing so.

Experimentally, Thratta flexes her shoulders, feeling her skin stretch against the scabs on her back. Once, carrying water from the fountain back to the house, she had broken the scabs and returned home with a bloodstained tunic. A neighbour was concerned enough to make enquiries of Thratta's mistress, something which caused some concern in the household, for any Athenian can launch a prosecution against a person who badly mistreats their slaves. That evening, Thratta was whipped on the backs of her thighs so as not to damage her back more obviously.

Athenian laws protecting slaves do not come out of concern for their welfare, but because if enough slaves are mistreated they might all rise together in rebellion – and slaves easily outnumber the free citizens in Athens. Technically, Thratta is listed as among her master's goods and chattels as an *anthropodo* – a human-footed beast rather than a four-legged one. Her worth is about 450 drachmae, or just under eight months of her master's income as foreman of a gang of slave construction workers. Most domestic slaves are considered valuable household tools and treated accordingly – but not all.

As she pushes her skinny body through the crowds thronging the narrow street, Thratta wonders how many of those jostling her are slaves like herself, with bruises like hers. Slaves in Athens have no distinctive markings or dress, so it is often difficult to distinguish slave from free. In her case, though, it is easy enough to make the distinction – like all women in Athens, Thratta keeps her hair tied back in a basic chignon, and this reveals to anyone who cares to look that she bears a horse tattoo, which rears

TATTOOS ON THE ARMS OF A THRACIAN WOMAN (LEFT)

from her collarbone up the side of her neck.

Doubtless that tattoo was a source of pride to the Thracian artist who so adorned the headman's daughter. Until the age of twelve, Thratta had been a little princess in her village on the banks of the River Strymon deep in the wild Thracian country east of Macedonia. She had never even heard of the Greeks until one day her village was filled with strange men in white linen armour who carried swords and clubs and wielded them with ruthless efficiency. Naturally the headman had been the raiders' first victim, and the last Thratta had seen of her father was a broken body lying in the dust, with hungry village dogs already circling the corpse.

At the island of Thasos, Thratta was separated from her

mother and shipped on to Delos, where she was part of a batch of slaves purchased by a wholesaler for resale in Athens. There, just as she had already lost her parents, she then lost her name. Her new owners called her Thratta – 'the Thracian' – and her horse tattoo went from a symbol of pride to being the mark of a barbarian, someone who was by nature a slave. As civilized folk, the Athenians do not tattoo their bodies.

Thratta, now sixteen, had last night dreamed of her home in Thrace – the wide river with its lush banks and the grey, snow-capped mountains rearing to the north. She remembered the sheep dotting the pastures and the flights of migratory storks marking the seasons overhead. Then she had awakened in her little alcove to the stink of excrement from the sewer-river Eridanus, which flowed past her owners' home, and had risen wearily before dawn to check the sourdough poolish that she would be baking into bread rolls for the evening.

Well, tool and chattel she might be, but what distinguishes Thratta from the broom and mop stacked in their crude shelter in the courtyard is that, unlike the other domestic tools, she can dream. And Thratta not only dreams of freedom, but has also been secretly working hard to turn those dreams into reality.

Domestic slaves are often freed, Thratta knows, even as she knows that her owners are more likely to beat or work her to death than to free her. But old Angitis, the vegetable farmer whose stall she will seek out at the Keremeikos market, was also once a slave. More than that, he is a Thracian and indignant about how Thratta is being treated. Sometimes, and hopefully again today, he will let Thratta have old, almost unsaleable produce for free and will add the two obols that Thratta's mistress gave her to the secret stash he has been keeping for his young friend.

By her own reckoning, Thratta needs 200 obols. She has seventy in her stash with Angitis, and there's 120 obols Thratta thinks she's owed by her mistress from the money she was not given for the shopping that she had to do anyway.

Thratta had always planned to run away, but her vague plans had suddenly turned to terrifying reality at the fish market yesterday. A casual encounter had turned into a long conversation with a fisherman whose ship had been blown west to Athens by a recent storm. As soon as they have patched up their boat, the fisherman and his crew intend to return to harvesting the bluefish that migrate south from the Bosphorus along the coast of Asia Minor past Halicarnassus, the fishermen's home port.

After repairing their boat, the fishermen need money, and for 100 obols they will overcome their scruples about taking women to sea and bring Thratta with them to Halicarnassus. The problem is that the fishermen must leave with the tide tomorrow, in the small hours of the morning. The season is getting late and the Aegean has become dangerously stormy, so if the little ship does not leave tomorrow it may not be able to leave at all. So right there and then in the fish market, Thratta had to make the biggest decision of her young life, and she is rather proud that she did not hesitate for a heartbeat.

Today, Thratta will collect her coins from Angitis, take her beating for the afternoon and in the dead of night she will sneak from the house and start the long walk to the Piraeus harbour where the fishing boat is moored. The dangers are obvious, and Thratta knows there's a good chance that the fishermen might simply rape the runaway and pitch her corpse overboard once they are out of sight of land. Yet Thratta feels she has to take that chance. The stoic philosophers say slaves are only slaves because they believe themselves to be. Well, if she is going to die tomorrow, at least she will die a free woman. Oh yes, and that little vase full of obols that her mistress has been collecting is coming along, too. Her mistress owes her at least that, and some fresh sea air will do the coins good.

The Sprinter

Symilos of Neapolis has not been home for almost a decade because getting there is both dangerous and unprofitable. He is not a wanted man but rather the opposite – he can count himself a favourite son of Naples and can expect a hero's welcome on whatever date he is able to return. Rather, the problem with any triumphant homecoming is the location of Symilos' native city, which is on the west coast of Italy. Naples is Greek – as Greek as Syracuse or Ephesus – but Naples it is a Greek colony in a barbarian land. And, for the past two decades, the dominant barbarians in Italy – the Romans – have been locked in a seemingly never-ending war with the Phoenician barbarians of North Africa and Sicily, the Carthaginians.

From the perspective of an Italian Greek [Greeks regard every non-Greek as a 'barbarian' by definition], it would be wonderful if Romans and Carthaginians either settled their differences or killed each other off and left the world at peace, but that is not likely to happen soon. One reason that these two nations hate each other so much is because they are very much alike. Both Romans and Carthaginians have acquired the accoutrements of civilization without the reasonableness that should have come as part of the package. While most Greek states would have settled matters amicably after a few seasons of stimulating warfare, Romans and Carthaginians have a kind of dour stubbornness that won't let them acknowledge that their war has gone on far longer than any sane Greek would consider reasonable. After non-stop killing for years, the struggle has become a grinding war of attrition that seems destined to end with the death of the last member of one or the other nation.

At present, Rome's long war is being fought out in the seas around Sicily, waters treacherous enough to discourage any traveller even without rival fleets patrolling the waves, arbitrarily stopping merchant ships and confiscating their cargoes. If a merchantman belongs to a nation allied with the warship that stopped it, the crew might be pressed into service at the oar (both nations are desperate for rowers); if the ship belongs to a neutral state, then the crew risk being enslaved or simply killed as an example of why one should not trade with the enemy.

Therefore, were he to try to return home to Naples, the athletic young Symilos might well find himself diverted to a new career – possibly as a rower for the Roman fleet or as a slave labourer in the olive groves of Tunis – and Symilos rather likes the career that he has.

Being of a somewhat philosophical bent, Symilos sometimes wonders if the honours and riches that the Neapolitans have showered upon him in his absence do not belong elsewhere. A lawmaker perhaps, whose laws, strong and just, knit together the social fabric of the city, a soldier who helps his people escape great peril or a doctor who labours through the dangers of a pandemic; such people have talents that benefit humanity. All that Symilos can do is run very, very fast over a short distance. Symilos is an Olympic-class sprinter.

In fact, it may well be that Symilos is the fastest man in the known world. The event in which he competes is called the *stadion*, a sprint of nearly 200 metres across the chariot-racing track of the same name (the distance varies slightly from venue to venue). Already Symilos is an iso-Olympic champion, for he was the victor of the most recent Games at the Ptolemeia. To listen to flatterers at the court of Ptolemy II, these Games, which the pharaoh instituted in honour of his late father Ptolemy I, have already surpassed the Olympics in grandeur and prestige. Ptolemy himself insists that his Games are the equal of the Olympics ['iso-' is a Greek prefix meaning 'the same as'], and he demands that champions at his Games receive the same honours from their native cities as do Olympic victors.

For a start, that means money – heaps of the stuff – a

statue in the agora (marketplace), free meals at the town hall for life and probably a nice pension at the end of it all. In short, the complete dream of wealth and fame, which is what propels all Greek athletes. That a man might compete in the Games as an amateur just for the love of the sport simply does not occur to Symilos. He is an athlete, and the very word 'athlete' means 'one who competes for a prize'. Even in the athletic events of legend, when the Greeks took time off from their siege of Troy, the prizes for the victors were iron spits, horses and captive women. After all, the humblest carpenter and most powerful general are both alike paid for their labour, so why should anyone expect less of an athlete who works harder and sacrifices more than those in most other professions?

At present, Symilos is gracing the home of a patron in Cyrene while he contemplates his next move. The patron is a wealthy aristocrat who is delighted to have Symilos on the premises to be shown off to guests, rather as a prizewinning stallion or a priceless work of art might be. In return, Symilos and his trainer get free food and lodging and the use of Cyrene's gymnasium whenever he needs it – which is often.

The question is not whether Symilos will compete in the Olympics, for he and everyone else takes this for granted. It is really a question of how best to prepare for the event, for Symilos will certainly not lack money. Already messages have come from his native city assuring him that Naples stands ready to fund his training, his trainer, a dietician, a masseur and whatever else Symilos might require. With all due respect to Ptolemy, his games and the 'iso-' prefix, nothing equals the Olympic Games or the glory that an Olympic champion bestows on his city, and Naples is prepared to make the investment for that glory.

Cities have been known to knock a breach through their own walls so that a returning Olympic victor need not demean himself by walking through a mere gate – and that is for winners of relatively minor events, such as the pentathlon. The oldest and the defining event of the Olympics is the *stadion*, the race in which Symilos excels. So honoured is this foot race that Olympiads – the entire five-year period, which includes the year of the Games themselves – are often referred to by the name of the winner of the *stadion* sprint. Yes, to have half a decade forever afterwards known as 'the Olympiad of Symilos of Naples' is something for which that city is prepared to pay whatever it takes.

Of course, Symilos' current host would prefer that his show athlete remained to enjoy the clement seaside air

ATHLETES COMPETE IN A FOOTRACE

of Cyrene while the running star slowly eases back into an Olympic training regime. But this probably will not happen. A sprinter who runs only against himself loses the edge that comes only from competition. This is a fact known not just to Symilos but also to his fellow top-class sprinters, and each of them will be making the same calculations that Symilos is working through at present: where to go, what events to attend and who else will be there?

Obviously, Symilos and his fellow athletes are keen to watch and size each other up as they compete in preliminary games before the Olympics. No one wants to peak early for these minor events and lose form by the time the big race comes around, yet at the same time no one wants the competition to get a psychological boost by thinking that a runner has lost his edge. It's a fine balance, further complicated by the fact that foot races can involve collisions and injuries, especially because no Olympic-class runner likes to lose, and a runner can easily overexert himself in winning an otherwise meaningless event.

To further complicate life, Symilos has been invited to compete at the games in Gortyn in Crete later this month. The messenger had broadly hinted that the city council of Gortyn had a proposition to put to him, which would make the trip well worth his while, and Symilos is curious to discover what that might be.

2

ΚΡΑΝΕΙΟΣ ΑΡΧΕΣ

(November – Beginnings)

〰〰〰〰〰〰〰〰〰〰〰〰〰〰〰〰〰〰

The Bride

'They go from Paidia to Artemis,' Athenian mothers sometimes remark as their female children come of age. Both Paidia and Artemis are goddesses, but appropriately enough Paidia is a minor goddess. She embodies playfulness and childish games while Artemis is a serious, grown-up goddess but – as is very important at this stage – Artemis is also a virgin.

Young Apphia certainly knows that 'going from Paidia to Artemis' is a literal journey, for just a few weeks ago she had stood solemnly in her playroom while her mother gathered up the toys, which had been the companions of Apphia's youth. There was the battered little toy horse on wheels that she had pushed up the ramparts of an imaginary Troy on numerous occasions, reinventing

Homer's *Iliad* in a narrative for the rag doll that had been with her since she was three. This doll had been carefully placed in a bag, along with Apphia's toy horse, rattles, spinning tops and other stuffed and carved animals.

Now Apphia, accompanied by her mother, had joined a group of other girls in a remarkably tedious ceremony at the temple of Artemis. Here, the girls' childhood toys have been dedicated to the goddess, with the ceremony serving as a formal statement that the participants are no longer children but women in their own right. Throughout the ceremony, Apphia has snuck glances at the other girls as she tries to guess their age. She has just turned fifteen and is by no means the oldest of those present – by her guess,

STATUE OF A GIRL DEDICATED TO ARTEMIS

the oldest is around sixteen. Yet all the girls had one thing in common: at some time in the past few weeks they had first menstruated and, for girls in Athens, menstruation signals the end of childhood.

Apphia is now an adult, and one who faces an uncertain future. Her name means 'increase' and that is exactly what her birth had done for the family's problems. She was fortunate, she knows, to have been born into a moderately wealthy and well-connected family. She was unfortunate, as she is often reminded, in being the youngest of four daughters. Sons inherit the family property and carry the family name into the world. Girls stay at home and bear children, but in any respectable family girls get married first, and any girl who wants a good marriage needs a good dowry.

Dowries are important for all sorts of reasons. Firstly, while giving a dowry is meant to be a private matter, everyone who's interested knows at least its approximate sum, and the prestige of those involved in the marriage rises or falls according to the size of the gift. Secondly, a dowry comes with the bride and it cannot be separated from her, so no matter what misfortunes might affect the marriage, the wife knows that she should have her dowry to fall back upon.

To complicate things further, while Apphia's family have been in Athens for two generations, they are not, and never will be, Athenians. The Athenians guard their citizenship jealously, and though their rules have become looser in recent years, a non-citizen woman who marries an Athenian citizen is in a precarious position, legally speaking. By and large, metics (foreign residents in Greek cities, see page 123) – especially metics who have been long-established in Athens – tend to marry among themselves, often without bothering to inform the authorities in their home cities where they are officially citizens.

Despite these difficulties, Apphia's three older sisters have already grown up and married. The real issue for Apphia is that her father is going to be hard-pressed to find yet another dowry for his final daughter. She lives constantly with the unspoken reproach that she was not born a boy and she has tried hard to compensate for a possibly small dowry by learning those skills – among them weaving, dance and household management – that husbands look for in a potential wife. It also helps that her three sisters have proven unexpectedly fecund and have astonished her father by birthing nearly a dozen children between them – almost all boys. That's the sort of track record in breeding that potential in-laws prize in a wife.

As an aside, it should be mentioned that Apphia is also maturing into a truly beautiful young woman, slender as a colt and with huge hazel eyes, flawless pale skin and tumbling locks of naturally blonde hair. Yet as one of her [considerably plainer] older sisters had remarked with a sniff, beauty is all very well in a concubine or a courtesan, but it is hardly the first thing that a man looks for in a wife. Good family, finances and fertility all come well ahead of mere looks, because if a male wants a comely bedmate, no one will criticise or comment if he looks elsewhere. A man with money can have plenty of beautiful female companionship, but he only gets to have one wife.

Even if good looks are not a consideration, it is normal that a potential husband will give considerable time and thought to assessing the qualities of the various young women whom his family and friends consider marriageable material. And, while Apphia can certainly dream of her ideal spouse, she also knows that she herself will have absolutely no say in the matter. That's up to her *Kyrios*, a word that usually means 'lord and master', but which here (without much difference in meaning) applies to her legal guardian, in this case her father. Apphia's father will decide whom and when she marries, and on what terms.

It is probable, but not certain, that at least Apphia will have a chance to meet her husband before she is married to him, even though this meeting will be less for the purpose of courtship than to allow the would-be bridegroom personally to inspect the goods before he commits himself. All of Apphia's sisters first met their husbands in this way, and each meeting was followed by weeks of gossiping and giggling in the women's quarters as the sisters candidly assessed their parent's choices.

Two things comfort Apphia for the present. She is still considered young, so her parents have at least another two years before their hunt for a husband gets desperate. Secondly, she has the experience and companionship of her sisters to draw upon. Though each now has a family of her own, the girls often visit one another to discuss domestic affairs and exchange tips on child-rearing. Whatever married life might bring, Apphia reasons, at least it will have few surprises.

The Builder

The gods created man, but can men create gods? The builder Meton ponders this question as, yet again, he goes over the numbers before his meeting with the Egyptian paymaster. The figures he has prepared represent his bid to be chosen to construct a temple at Olympia for the god Serapis.

But is Serapis a real god? Or is he an invention of the Egyptian propaganda machine, created specifically for the purpose of uniting Egyptians and the Greek settlers within that country while simultaneously boosting Egyptian prestige abroad?

One thing is certain – though Serapis might have had a tenuous existence before Ptolemy I of Egypt plucked him from obscurity, the god certainly did not enjoy the Mediterranean fame and thousands of devoted worshippers that he has today.

Meton himself is a henotheist – that is, one who accepts the existence of other gods but who personally confines his worship to a single deity. For Meton, that deity is the Lady, the grey-eyed goddess Athena, especially in her aspect as Athena Ergane, the goddess of craftsmen and craftswomen. As a consequence, Meton worries less than he otherwise might about building a place of worship for this new god even though Serapis seems to claim some of the attributes usually given to Hades, the lord of the Underworld. Surely Meton's dedication to Athena will protect him from the

THE NEW OLD GOD SERAPIS

When the Macedonian warlord Ptolemy I took control of Egypt, he needed to show his new subjects that he was a traditional Egyptian pharaoh and the Greeks that he was as Greek as anyone. One way that Ptolemy squared the circle was through one of the most ancient of Egyptian cults – the veneration of the sacred Apis bull. When an Apis bull died, it was worshipped as a god, and Ptolemy built upon this by Greekifying the name of this god from 'Osiris-Apis' to 'Serapis'. Serapis was in many ways a customized god. Ptolemy wanted a uniquely Egyptian god who could not be immediately conflated with any existing member of the Greek pantheon, yet who had attributes of several. Unlike the famously animal-headed gods of Egypt, Serapis had a human head, and worship of this more Greek-style god was aggressively promoted elsewhere in the Hellenistic world. This worship was helpful to Ptolemaic propaganda because Serapis and the goddess Isis were identified as the protectors and benefactors of the pharaoh. The main temple of the god in Egypt, the Serapeum in Alexandria, was one of the greatest temples in the ancient world, and it stood until AD 391 when a Christian mob destroyed it as a stronghold of paganism.

Relief showing Athena resting her arm on a pillar

jealousy of Hades? The devout builder certainly hopes so, even though the cult statue he will be placing in the temple might, in some opinions, verge upon blasphemy.

Since Meton is bidding for the contract to build the temple of Serapis, unsurprisingly he has given much consideration to the effigy of the god, which will be located in the *naos*, the central inner chamber and the most sacred part of the building. The sculpture Meton commissions will be based upon the infamous statue of Serapis, which originally stood in Sinope, a city on the shores of the Euxine [the Black Sea]. This depicts the god as a male with Greek features but clad in clothing with Egyptian trappings. That

Serapis has human features is alone enough to distinguish him from many Egyptian gods, which have the heads of sacred animals, yet the statue that Meton plans to recreate also has a basket upon his head and a three-headed hound at his feet. The three-headed beast is a clear reference to the Underworld, the gates of which are guarded by the three-headed hound Cerberus. Yet the symbolically literate Greeks will also pick up on the basket, which is used to hold grain and is therefore an acknowledged sign of death and rebirth [because grain falls to the ground and arises a season later as a new plant]. Hades might not be too happy with that.

This statue is almost as well known as the god it represents, which is why, despite the Hadean attributes, Meton wants to flatter the Egyptians by using a reproduction if it. The story goes that Ptolemy I dreamed that the god wanted this sculpture in the massive new temple that the pharaoh was building for him in Alexandria. Yet all that Ptolemy's dream revealed was the description of the statue and its surroundings. Ptolemy was not even aware that such a sculpture really existed until one of his courtiers recognized the description and told the pharaoh of its location in the city of Sinope.

A team was immediately sent to purchase the statue, but the people of Sinope were unreasonably reluctant to part with it. Eventually, the protracted negotiations ended when the Egyptians set sail with the statue aboard their ship. According to the Egyptians, the god Serapis was frustrated by the delay and his statue had simply got off its pedestal and walked to the Egyptian ship. According to the people of Sinope, the Egyptians had descended

THE GREEKS IN EGYPT

Anyone who knows the tale of Oedipus and the riddle of the Sphinx will also know that ancient Greek and Egyptian history were closely intertwined. This was especially true during the Ptolemaic era, when Egypt was ruled by a Macedonian dynasty that actively encouraged the immigration of Greeks and the founding of entire Greek cities within Egypt. One thing that made this possible was the institution of the Greek *polis*, which was Greek culture encapsulated within a self-contained city in a model that spread, with only minor local variations, across the Greek world from Spain to Afghanistan. For example, archaeologists have unearthed a traditional Greek gymnasium at Watfa, the site of the ancient city of Philoteris, which was founded by Ptolemy II some 200 km (124 miles) south of the main centre of Greek Egypt at Alexandria. Greek culture continued to thrive in Egypt under the Roman empire and has left a rich heritage of papyrus texts, sculptures and paintings, but faded away after the Muslim conquest in AD 640.

upon the Serapis by night with block and tackle, and had blatantly stolen him away. Either way, Meton wants a copy of that statue in his proposed temple.

Given the energy and resources that the Ptolemaic kings have dedicated to spreading the worship of their 'new' god, it is perhaps no surprise that Ptolemy II has decided that he needs this temple of Serapis at that most Greek of all places – the sacred precinct of Olympia where the Olympic Games are held.

Well, that's not going to happen because the city fathers of Elis indignantly rejected the idea of a new god jostling for space in the already crowded temple precinct. Meton suspects that the Egyptians were never really serious about building in the sacred precinct itself, but only made the suggestion to soften the city fathers to the idea that the building might be constructed elsewhere in Olympia. After all, the precinct houses that temple with the ivory and gold statue of Zeus by the great sculptor Phydias. This statue is one of the wonders of the [ancient] world – and even the massive resources of the kingdom of Egypt would be hard put to compete with *that.*

Instead, the rather ingenious solution has been to purchase a plot of private land from a farmer whose fields adjoin the site at Olympia. Built on a small outcrop on the base of Mount Kronos, the new temple might not outshine the famous one to Zeus within the sacred precinct, but it will look down upon it.

Due to its literally prominent location, the temple must be as handsome a specimen of Greek sacred architecture as can be constructed within the (very generous) budget allocated. For this reason, Meton has consulted closely with architects from as far afield as Athens and Ephesus, and he now has three carefully constructed scale models to showcase different temple designs.

To an outsider, these designs might look almost identical,

but that is because the conventions of temple-building do not allow for a great deal of flexibility. For example, a temple built in the Doric style must have a fixed relationship between the proportions of the central *naos*, which houses the gods, and the number of columns in the *peristasis*, the colonnade that surrounds the *naos*. The location of other architectural features and their proportions relative to one another are also fixed, giving all temples throughout the Greek world a very similar appearance.

No matter that many of the building conventions go back to the Archaic era, when temples were built from wood, and the width of a building was limited by the number of timbers that could be laid across the roof, or that certain features are now purely ornamental, such as the pegs once used to secure these wooden beams. That's the way that the gods like their temples, and Serapis, who has broken so many rules already, will have no wish to damage his quest for acceptability further by breaking more. So, the temple will be very conventional.

Meton wants to persuade the Egyptian paymaster to go for a Doric-style temple because the style is plainer, and Meton can therefore build something grander with the same budget. He is well aware that the costs of even a small temple are mind-boggling, so keeping expenses down is one of his priorities.

Consider, for example, that the cost of a single plain Doric column is around 50,000 drachmae, and that the skilled workmen carving the columns might earn that amount in two lifetimes. Even Meton's most modest proposal has twelve of these columns, and if the Egyptian opts for the Ionian style, the cost of each column goes up to 65,000 drachmae due to the stylized column capitals and the fluting that must be meticulously carved into each column drum (where one slip of a chisel might cost 10,000 drachmae).

Yet it is those same costs that make Meton so eager to win the contract. Even if he takes a personal commission of 0.5 per cent of the upfront price, he never need worry about money again. As he paces the floor and waits for his potential patron to arrive, Meton dreams of retirement to his home island of Melos, and of the house he will build there for himself and his family.

〰〰〰〰〰〰〰〰〰〰〰〰〰〰〰〰〰〰〰〰〰

The Merchant

Whether one calls it Apollonopolis or Edfu, the huge temple city on the River Nile is a lot further south than the trader Sakion is comfortable with being. In normal times, Sakion likes to stay in Alexandria, buying and selling goods as they come in from the barbarian West and civilized East and making a profit on the traffic in either direction.

Spices, silks and sandals come from the East – how far east Sakion has no idea, for he only gets to know of the goods when they arrive at the port of Arsinoe on the shores of the Erythraean [Red] Sea. Given the uncertainties of life and trade, it is an unfortunate fact that deals sometimes fall through. Say the merchant who contracted to buy a cargo of Indian pepper has died or gone bankrupt, or the pepper was mysteriously 'acquired' by the well-armed crew of a ship from the famously piratical port of Raithos – suddenly there is an orphan cargo looking for a buyer. This is where Sakion steps in, acquiring the cargo and finding a new buyer for it.

As a Greek trader from a family long established in Egypt, Sakion has a web of contacts across the Hellenistic world, and he knows which buyers are likely to pay top prices for what products. If the goods are of sufficient value, Sakion will accompany them himself and personally make the sale while simultaneously renewing the personal contacts upon which his livelihood depends.

The kingdom of Kush, a distant land to the south of Egypt, had hardly registered as a feature on Sakion's trade interests until three months ago, when suddenly it became of major importance. A fellow merchant had spent most of the year negotiating a major trade deal with businessmen in Meroë, one of the principal cities of Kush, and then, with the deal done and the contracts signed and witnessed, the merchant had perished in an early autumn storm while bringing a shipload of Spanish silver to Alexandria.

The merchant's wife had contacted Sakion, asking if he was interested in taking up the contract. Sakion's initial lack of interest quickly dissipated when he discovered the nature of the goods involved – twelve talents (700 kg or 1,540 lb) of raw ivory, going for a bargain price – just at the moment when the Attalid king of Pergamon in Asia Minor is desperately seeking ivory to embellish the temples and monuments of his growing city.

The Kushites had arranged to deliver the ivory to a middleman at Elephantine, on the upper reaches of the Nile, and the middleman had contracted to bring the goods almost half the way of their journey to Apollonopolis/ Edfu. There, the ivory needs to be collected and paid for, so to the ancient sandstone city Sakion has had to go. It was not an easy trip, for it involved battling upstream along the Nile the entire way, a journey of some 5,400 *stades* (just over 1,000 km or 600 miles). Also, every *stade* past the city of Memphis, Sakion could feel the hostility of the native Egyptians growing, and this makes him extremely uncomfortable.

Egypt is an ancient land, and one with a proud history. A thousand years before Alexander the Great, Egypt traded with the Assyrians and ruled parts of the Levant. Five hundred years ago, Egypt had been ruled by Kushite kings – which is one reason why today Kushite merchants are uncomfortable venturing further north than Elephantine.

The Egyptians prefer to think of themselves as conquerors rather than as the conquered, and they have monuments packed with bas-reliefs showing their rulers doing the conquering. As a result, they resent reminders of past and present humiliations, be these traders from the upstart Greek city of Alexandria or merchants from the ancient kingdom of Kush. Overall, southern Egypt and its sullen, mutinous folk is an uncomfortable place to be doing business.

As a trader, Sakion is used to handling goods that have travelled almost unimaginable distances. He remembers meeting a merchant from India who informed him that his cargo of spices had travelled even further in reaching India than it would go onward to its final point of sale in Greece. Yet, even so, the city of Meroë, from which his ivory will be coming, seems to Sakion both far away and fabulous.

They say that Napata, the capital of Kush, has more pyramids than Egyptian Thebes, and that Meroë is a populous city of towering buildings surrounded by lush forest. Ironwork from Meroë is as famous for its quality as for its scarcity, for it is a rare trader who will haul such heavy and relatively inexpensive goods 2,500 km (1,550 miles) north to Alexandria. But diamonds, leopard skins, exotic animals and yes, ivory, can and do often make the trip, though it is almost unheard of for one merchant to travel with the product from start to finish. Like the spices that Sakion imports from the East, the goods are passed from merchant to merchant. Often, those who finally buy the goods are completely ignorant of the people and the places from which their purchase originated.

Now, ensconced in a guest house overlooking the Nile, Sakion spends his evenings discussing theatre with his Greek host, or regaling the man with his tales of travel through Greece and the Orient. He spends his days prowling the walkways beside the docks, nervously waiting for news that his precious cargo is headed down the river towards him.

At such moments, Sakion wonders about the rest of Africa and its brown-skinned inhabitants. The peoples of the Mediterranean know of the kingdom of Kush because both Kush and Egypt share the long artery of the River Nile, up and down which trade and information flow constantly. Yet

Africa is vast, and completely unknown, for west of Egypt the impenetrable sands of the Sahara stretch all the way to the shores of the ocean beyond the Mediterranean. What lies west of the Nile, south of the Sahara? What unknown kingdoms and civilizations flourish and trade, their people and culture unknown to the lands further north?

As a Greek and an Egyptian, Sakion knows with unshakeable certainty that his land and culture are superior to anything in the world. But now that he has been made aware of the huge unknown land to the south, his curiosity has been piqued. Perhaps it might be worth chartering a barge and travelling a bit further upriver to meet his cargo halfway. Along the riverbank there will be crocodiles, ibises and hippopotami, even perhaps the first pale pink flamingoes arriving on their northern migration. Such an adventurous trip will surely be better than lurking in the shadows of the gloomy temples of Edfu and the city's shifty, sullen people.

The Lyre Player

When she gets back to her rooms, Kallia carefully unwraps the instrument that has cost almost half of her savings. It's a lyre, a replacement for the one that leans against her bed, still useable but useless as a professional musical instrument thanks to the heat of the Anatolian summer. So Kallia has had to find a replacement, and this required some careful selection.

Not all lyres are created equal – there's the *phorminx* lyre, which is still played by bards in villages where sheep are the economic mainstay, and the quaint but impractical *chelys*, which legend says was the very first lyre ever invented.

The *chelys* gets its name from the tortoise, which was sacrificed by the god Hermes to create the instrument. Hermes was at the time guarding a fine herd of cattle that he had stolen from Apollo. To pass the time, the young god (who was a remarkably precocious infant) took a set of horns from the skull of an antelope and used this as the frame for a set of strings. Plucking the strings produced a pleasant sound, but one which lacked vibrancy, so Hermes emptied a tortoise out of his home and used the shell as a sound board to add the missing depth.

Right now, Kallia rather wishes she had brought a *chelys* with her to Anatolia. The original *chelys* lyre, however, requires the happy serendipity of a tortoise with just the right thickness and flexibility of its shell to work perfectly with the set of antelope horns that it is paired with (and Kallia sometimes wonders how many tortoises and antelopes one must get through to obtain a perfect match).

Of course, one can get around the problem by using something other than tortoise and antelope. So, like any professional lyre player, Kallia uses a *kithara*, which, like the *phorminx*, is a box harp, though otherwise the *kithara* is to the *phorminx* what a thoroughbred racing stallion is to the mule that pulls a dung-cart.

A box harp eliminates gratuitous cruelty to tortoises and takes the random element out of harp-making by the

Female lyre player with a *kithara*

careful construction of a hollow wooden box that does the same job as a tortoise shell but with far greater precision. Careful carpentry can form the box into a sounding board, which shapes and gives texture to the vibration of the strings. Depending on the wood, the thickness and the overall shape of a sounding board, the same string might sound mellow, loud and resonant or tremulous when plucked.

Kallia's original *kithara* was of cherry wood, and all the more expensive for that, as luthiers very much dislike working with the hard and brittle cherry. Furthermore, cherry sapwood and heartwood have different textures and a craftsman can only usually work with one or the other, not least because the two parts of the same log age differently. A lyre with combined woods quickly develops a blotchy appearance, and a faint dissonance lurks under the rich, clear notes of the soundboard.

The other problem with cherry wood is that the tree grows in well-watered places with high relative humidity. So if a luthier uses wood that has not been comprehensively dried to the aridity of the Sahara in midsummer, then only an unwise kitharist will take her instrument on a tour of the Anatolian highlands. Kallia was one such person, and she discovered to her deep distress that the wood of her instrument had been imperfectly dried. And so, in the baking heat of the Anatolian plateau, the lyre began to shrink, the drying wood warping slightly as the *kithara* literally tried to tear itself apart.

What remains now, propped against the bed, is still a useable instrument capable of being played to good effect

– if one is entertaining a market-day crowd or a party of soldiers standing down at the end of the campaigning season. Sadly, though, the instrument is no longer fit for its intended purpose – the entertainment of aristocratic connoisseurs in the small, acoustically perfect auditoriums designed specifically for artistic performances. (Such auditoriums are dedicated to Apollo and known as *odeons*.)

It is a mark of good breeding in the Greek world for an aristocrat to have expertise, if not in the playing of the lyre, then at least in the appreciation of such music. Kallia is paid top wages for her appearances because her listeners expect expert performance on a quality instrument – and Kallia's old lyre is no longer such a piece.

Still, the lyre will at least sell for a decent sum because Kallia has enough of a reputation that just owning one of her old instruments is something of a cachet, and most aristocratic strummers have so many flaws of their own that the more subtle defects in the warped *kithara* will pass unnoticed in the general cacophony. Alternatively, Kallia might sell the lyre to her current patron, a councillor in the city of Eusebia, whose children she is currently failing to teach the fine art of lyre playing.

Legend has it that while Heracles was a highly proficient archer, he was downright useless with any other stringed instrument. Still, since the young Heracles was an aristocratic youth being raised in highly cultured Thebes, his parents had to make the attempt to teach him. For this challenging task they picked the best person available – a man called Linus of Thrace. Linus shared the musical talent of his brother Orpheus (the best musician ever known), which was not surprising since his parents were Apollo and Calliope, chief of the Muses.

Kallia herself has sung a few of the lugubrious dirges called *linoi* after Linus, who tragically died in action. That is, exasperated by his pupil's ham-fisted attempts to carry a tune, Linus smacked Heracles over the head in frustration. Heracles was equally frustrated, and he went from murdering the melody to murdering his teacher with a single muscular swipe of the lyre. (Which, the professional Kallia notes, probably did not do the lyre much good either.)

While her current pupils lack the muscles and ill-temper of the young Heracles, they probably surpass even his musical inability. The two boys cannot carry a tune in a bucket, and their sister is only slightly better. The girl is approaching adolescence, and both her passionate stare and the intensity of her playing suggest to Kallia that the girl is taking the verses of Sappho of Lesbos a bit too literally for her teacher's comfort.

So now, as she unwraps her new instrument with slightly trembling hands, Kallia decides that she has dallied long enough in the pleasant backwater of Eusebia. Like herself, the luthier who made her new lyre has decided that his talent needs a larger and more appreciative clientele, so he is packing his shop and moving to Pergamon. Kallia will tender her resignation tomorrow and accompany him. At least that way, if there are any problems with her new instrument, she will have no difficulty in taking up the matter with the manufacturer.

3

ΛΑΝΟΤΡΟΠΙΟΣ ΠΡΟΕΤΟΙΜΑΣΙΕΣ

(December – Preparations)

The Farmer

The rain falls in hissing silver sheets across the fields, and Mount Kronos is hidden behind the resulting veil. Iphita, arms akimbo, stands beneath the shelter of the porch and watches with angry relief. Finally! All through the previous month the clouds had taunted her – heavy and black, rolling in from the Ionian Sea only to disperse inland after only a few spots of rain. Now, at last, the rain has come, heavy and drenching, saturating the soil and loosening the hard crust of baked earth that has covered the fields since the summer drought. Ploughing is at last possible.

Not that the previous month was spent in idleness. Even before the Pleiades had dipped below the horizon, Iphita's workers had started their preparations. Sickles

BASE OF VASE SHOWING ACTIVITY IN
THE PLOUGHING SEASON

were sharpened, and a line of men had moved across field after field, stripping off the summer's weeds and grass. The mass was loaded on to a wagon and now sits behind the barn, where the pouring rain will help to decompose it into a steaming pile that will be mixed with dried dung and human excrement before it returns to the fields as compost. From such insalubrious origins eventually come the housewife's fresh-baked sweetcakes and savoury buns.

Then the holm-oak plough tree was fetched from storage, and wooden dowels were affixed to the sides of the heavy pole and the share-pole attached. The plough tree has the metal-tipped ploughshare at one end, and the oxen will be hitched to the oaken share-pole at the other. For weeks now, the oxen have been fed grain and regularly exercised, for the time of ploughing will leave them comprehensively worn out by each day's end.

Iphita has also checked that the spare plough is in working order, for it is not uncommon for a plough to splinter to pieces under the stress of breaking the hard earth. Nor is it unusual for Iphita's less provident neighbours to come begging for that spare plough, which she finds it politic to lend, especially since she will under no circumstances lend out her oxen. Not since a neighbouring farmer once returned the beasts slavered with sweat, striped with whip marks, exhausted and almost lame. Fortunately, this is a busy time of year on every farm, and Iphita's ingenious excuses as to why she can't spare her oxen have got the message across, so now the neighbours no longer even bother to ask.

Meanwhile, Iphita's labourers have been clearing the brushwood within her treasured stand of oak trees, and from the larger offcuts these men have each fashioned a 'beetle', a crudely shaped mallet with which they will follow the plough and break up large clods of earth. Because this year will be a late ploughing, the sower will follow immediately behind those breaking the earth, and behind him will come a lad armed with a slingshot. Those birds that think to make a meal of the seed freshly scattered on the newly broken ground will end up as a meal themselves. It's not just turtle doves and sand grouse that come to plunder Iphita's crop – moorhens and partridges also try and later join the farmworkers at dinner.

Despite the late sowing, Iphita has gambled on emmer wheat in her fields. In a normal year, she would have opted for barley even though this sells for less, because December wheat is harvested late. Therefore, if a late-sown wheat crop is to produce a harvest comparable to that from an early sowing, one needs a wet, grey spring. Iphita has nothing against flower buds and cuckoos but come next spring she wants gloomy skies and drizzle. Should the spring come dry and sunny, however, and the wheat harvest is meagre in consequence, the farm's finances will not suffer. This is an Olympic year, and the farmworkers are now as adept at milking tourists as they are at milking their goats. So if it is going to be a profitable year no matter what, why not gamble on making the year even more profitable still?

This thought reminds Iphita to check that the goats are still actually producing plentiful milk (tourists like goat's-milk cheese). The milk supply from some of the younger does has dropped off, and this, accompanied by tail-wagging and vigorous vocalization, suggests that it is time for the does to be bred. She has to allow a gestation period of around 150 days, then this will be followed by birth and a full milk supply by spring. Then, after another three months for a brine-aged cheese to reach maturity, Olympian sports lovers will be treated to a first-rate product. Indeed, the farm markets Iphita's cheese under the wordy slogan 'As fine a delicacy as ever produced since Aristaios [the son of Apollo] taught cheese-making to humanity.'

Talking of breeding … Iphita frowns as she recalls her most recent discussion with her son. Last week he had accepted her invitation to dinner at the farm (which is a polite way of saying he was too terrified to refuse her summons). The topic of grandchildren had come up during the meal – and also beforehand, and well after the last honey cakes had been consumed. From her somewhat isolated position out on the farm, Iphita has nonetheless been busy over the past two months, rounding up a series of eligible young women from the neighbours and her contacts in Elis, and sending them to meet her son at carefully contrived social occasions. All to no avail.

It is infuriating. If Iphita were a man she could simply select a suitable wench from a neighbouring farm, discuss with her father what fields the bride would acquire as a dowry, and inform her son that he was about to become a husband. It's much more complicated for a woman because, technically speaking, Iphita is the ward and dependant of that same useless lump that she is trying to marry off. And her son, usually so compliant, is proving unexpectedly stubborn in matters matrimonial. Indeed, the lad has now decided that he is off to Athens to study Epicurean philosophy – which would only be true if Epicureanism taught the importance of getting as far from one's parent and potential spouses as humanly possible.

All is not lost, though. Iphita's family has long maintained *Xenia* – the tradition of guest-friendship – with an Elean family in Athens. Should that family attend the Olympics, they are welcome guests at the farm. Should business or pleasure take Iphita's clan to Athens, they stay at the home of their Xenos (guest-friend). It's a useful arrangement, especially since discreet enquiries have ascertained that their Athenian Xenos has a daughter who has recently come of marriageable age. Usually, a girl living in Athens would be expected to marry someone from the same city, but perhaps the parents can be persuaded to make an exception for a long-standing family ally from their ancestral homeland. The girl is the youngest of four sisters, so her dowry will be pitiful – but at this point Iphita would happily marry her child to the daughter of an Illyrian pirate, if only the girl were fertile and acceptable to her fastidious son.

The Diplomat

As he sits in his study contemplating the snow-covered rooftops of Pella, Persaeus also has marriage in mind. Not his own, for the Macedonian diplomat has been living comfortably with his plump concubine for almost a decade now, and he has no intention of changing his cozy domestic arrangements. No, the marriage that he is contemplating is the unhappy union of the Seleucid king Antiochus II and the daughter of Ptolemy II of Egypt.

It has long been of considerable annoyance to Macedon that the nation's nemesis, Ptolemy II, has placed his offspring directly into the line of succession of the large and powerful Seleucid empire. The Seleucid king did not have a lot of choice about marrying Ptolemy's daughter because, after a long and difficult war with Egypt, he had been faced with either acquiring a new wife or losing a substantial chunk of his kingdom. Accordingly, and very reluctantly, Antiochus had divorced his current wife and married Ptolemy's daughter.

THE REAL PERSAEUS

Born around 310 BC, Persaeus was of aristocratic stock. The writer Diogenes Laertius tells us he was fond of music and parties. When King Antigonus II of Macedon invited the great philosopher Zeno to his court, Zeno sent his student Persaeus in his stead. Persaeus became a trusted member of the court, though Antigonus once tested his stoic ideals by informing him that his estates in Citium had been destroyed. Seeing his courtier's distress, Antigonus remarked that material things evidently mattered to Persaeus after all. Persaeus' last mission for Antigonus was to take charge of Corinth and hold it against the nascent Achaean League. He died defending the city when it was attacked by Aratus of Sikyon.

Neither the Macedonians nor the ex-wife of the Seleucid king were at all happy with this arrangement. Nor, according to reports coming from Macedonian spies in the Seleucid royal court, is Antiochus currently particularly content with his bride. There are reports of screaming matches in the royal bedchamber and the king is spending as much time away from the capital as possible – not that it is difficult for the ruler of a slowly collapsing empire to find excuses that will keep him from enjoying wifely company.

There is much debate in the royal courts of the Hellenistic world as to whether the Seleucid king will

ANTIOCHUS OF SELEUCIA, FROM A CONTEMPORARY COIN

renege on his marriage deal with Ptolemy and go back to his fuming former wife. Needless to say, the Macedonians would love for this to happen. Not only would it put the Ptolemaic nose severely out of joint – in itself a worthwhile end – but also the focus of Ptolemy's mischief-making would swing away from Greece and back to the Seleucid empire.

For that reason, the Macedonian king recently summoned Persaeus and instructed him to travel to Seleucia. Once within the Seleucid empire, Persaeus is to track down Antiochus and offer him Macedon's full support should the king choose to switch wives once more. Given the difficulties of midwinter travel, by the time Persaeus meets Antiochus the man will be busy with plans and preparations for the coming spring. At the start of the new campaigning season, the Seleucid monarch must decide whether to attempt to deal with secessionist rebels to the east, the troublesome people of Armenia and Anatolia, or – should he opt to reset his matrimonial arrangements – face the wrath of a disgruntled Ptolemy. The job of Persaeus is to persuade Antiochus that dealing with Ptolemy should be his prime consideration.

The winter conditions mean that careful arrangements are needed. Were it springtime, Persaeus would simply take a barge to Pella's seaport and travel by ship to the harbour of Seleucia Pieria at the mouth of the Orontes river. (Persaeus' adopted home city of Pella itself used to be a seaport, but the harbour is now a silted-up marsh.) But midwinter, sailing over the stormy seas of Ionia is little more than an elaborate way of committing suicide, so instead the diplomat must travel east through the wild lands of Thrace, across the Hellespont at Byzantium and then make his way south through Asia Minor.

It's going to be a long, uncomfortable trip, but at least it will give Persaeus the opportunity to report back to his royal master the true state of affairs in such places as Pergamon and Ancyra, where he will stop over on his travels. It's also a good idea for a senior diplomat to get out in the field once in a while. No one likes to be the bearer of bad news, so by and large the reports reaching the Macedonian court tend to have an unrealistically optimistic bias to them. By getting out of the capital and seeing things for himself, Persaeus will be able to give his king more accurate intelligence when he gets back.

Sighing, Persaeus pulls a sheet of papyrus toward himself. It's all very well for the king to decide he needs to send a diplomat to Seleucia; now that diplomat has to sit down with his staff and make some serious arrangements. Firstly, there are deputies to brief on their duties while their master is away; there are messengers to sort out so that Persaeus is kept up to speed with developments at home; and other messengers to be sent ahead to the cities and kingdoms that Persaeus will be passing through on his way to Seleucia. No one will be particularly happy to have a senior representative of one of the great Hellenistic powers turn up unexpectedly on their doorstep, so Persaeus needs to give them time to prepare – he's meant to be spreading goodwill as he goes along, after all.

Then there's also the matter of his entourage. As the representative of Macedon, Persaeus can't arrive looking like some bedraggled, road-weary tramp. He'll need a good wardrobe and people to maintain it. He will need cooks for those times he must stop at the side of the road and, above all, a substantial cavalry bodyguard to make sure he is not relieved of his valuables or even his life while en route to his destination. And, once again, all this needs to be cleared with the independent cities and small kingdoms he will pass through lest the sudden arrival of a substantial number of Macedonian cavalrymen give the wrong impression.

Hopefully all will go well. The diplomatic train will roll smoothly through Asia Minor leaving behind friends and allies, and Persaeus will find the Seleucid king at or near his capital. The man will be deeply disillusioned with his Egyptian wife and ready and willing to return to the bosom of the family he was forced to abandon for diplomatic reasons.

The next question is, where should Persaeus go from there? Greece remains a bubbling cauldron of discontent, so if all goes successfully with the Seleucid king Antiochus, it might not be a bad idea to cross back through the Aegean Sea and return via Athens and Thessaly. At the back of his mind, Persaeus also has the idea that he would like to extend his trip somehow to take in the Peloponnese later in the year. Despite his new mission, he has not entirely given up the idea of making it to the Olympic Games.

ⓖⓖⓖⓖⓖⓖⓖⓖⓖⓖⓖⓖⓖⓖⓖⓖⓖⓖⓖⓖⓖ

The Runaway

As happens in most Greek cities, the city council of Halicarnassus regularly posts notices in the agora asking for information leading to the capture of an escaped slave. The bounty on Hermon's head is three talents of copper – but only two if the escapee has taken refuge in a temple, from which he must be winkled out without offending the god from whom he has claimed sanctuary.

A small group stands before the posted list of announcements while a helpful citizen reads them aloud for the benefit of those present who cannot read. Among these is a skinny boy just approaching adolescence who stands at the back of the group. The lad's features are modestly shadowed by a hooded cloak, which provides him with both anonymity and shelter from the chilly winter wind.

As yet, there has been no sign of the notice that Thratta has been dreading. Something along the lines of 'Thratta, an escaped slave girl, aged eighteen, with straw-blonde hair and a horse tattoo on her neck. She has taken with her forty drachmae of coin and may also be recognized by her scars from whippings for insolence and disobedience.'

Thratta knows it is only a matter of time before such a notice is issued. Once a slave has gone missing, the indignant owners report the runaway to the city authorities and a description of the escapee is taken, along with details of what reward the slave-owner is prepared to offer. Then lists of escaped slaves are circulated around the cities and towns of the Hellenistic world, to be read with interest by local people who tend to regard finding an escaped slave in their midst as the equivalent of winning a prize in the lottery.

Thratta has heard of professional slavecatchers, but her careful research has shown that these are usually commissioned for the pursuit of slaves who have helped themselves to a substantial portion of their master's wealth before decamping. (Hermon, Thratta notes, got away with a stash of gold coins and some pearls, which might make him of some interest to a bounty hunter with time on his hands. Since the notice has apparently been amended to show an increased reward, it seems that so far Hermon's getaway has been encouragingly successful.)

Fear of being recognized and hauled back to face the vindictive wrath of her sadistic owners casts a constant shadow over Thratta's days. It's a pity really, because otherwise she would honestly admit to having the time of her life. At first, the fishermen who had spirited her from Athens had been superstitiously apprehensive about having a female on board. But clear skies, clement winds and an abundant haul of bluefish had convinced the men that the gods approved of their actions. Actually, Thratta had contributed somewhat to the bluefish catch by scampering up the mast like a monkey and calling to the men below when she saw the dark shadows of the fish beneath the waves.

By the time the fishing boat had made harbour in Halicarnassus, Thratta was something of a mascot to the crew, who appreciated her cheerful demeanour (it is now weeks since anyone has hit her) and her readiness to pitch in to help with the numerous little jobs needed to keep a vessel in good order on the autumnal seas. Once the fishermen made harbour, a quick discussion among the crew resulted in Thratta disguising her sex and becoming the pre-adolescent nephew of a fishmonger's wife, a herbalist from Cilicia.

She now has a tiny room above a tailor's shop along the busy road that runs between the temple of Demeter and the necropolis outside the eastern city gate. The location is convenient for the harbour – a huge bay around which the crescent-shaped city is built. It's Thratta's job to rise before dawn each morning and hurry to the wharf where the fishermen are unloading their overnight catch. By now, Thratta can tell at a glance whether the fishermen have caught anchovies, pilchards or mullet in their nets – or even the occasional bonito, prized as a local delicacy when grilled or baked.

Thratta reports her findings to her 'uncle' who in turn will make his way to the docks to purchase the more attractive catches of the day, which Thratta has scouted for him. Some of the fish will be delivered directly to the houses of the wealthy who live on the hill between the theatre and the stoa of Ptolemy, and the trader will sell the remainder of the fish at his stall at the market. After completing her dawn duty, Thratta reports to her 'aunt', who sets her to various tasks, such as sorting or drying herbs, or mixing them into various concoctions, and this takes up the remainder of the morning.

For the rest of the day, Thratta is free to explore the city. Admittedly, Halicarnassus is not as great as it once was, back in the days when Queen Artemisia was determined to make her city the jewel of Anatolia. Halicarnassus has never fully recovered from rough handling when Alexander the Great conquered the place from the Persians, for when he realized the city was lost, the Persian commander had burned down much of it out of spite. Nor have things been helped by a recent minor earthquake. As a result, the famed Mausoleum built a century previously is showing signs of wear and tear, for all that it remains one of the wonders of the world.

One of the things Thratta most likes about Halicarnassus is that the city is protected by the Ptolemaic kingdom of Egypt, which blunts the reach of Macedon-dominated Athens in the matter of reclaiming escaped slaves and much besides. Ptolemy has been good for the city, building

QUEEN ARTEMISIA INSPECTS HER HUSBAND'S MAUSOLEUM

or restoring many civic buildings including the stoa, which bears his name. His rule is so light as to hardly merit the title, a fact for which the people of the city are duly grateful.

Overall, Thratta is well aware that her flight from Athens could have gone much, much worse. She has a home, people who seem friendly, if not overly concerned about her welfare, a place to sleep and all the fish she can eat. As welcoming a sanctuary as Halicarnassus may be, it is only a temporary refuge. After a while, people are going to wonder why the pre-adolescent boy remains beardless and why his voice never breaks. Come summer it will be almost impossible to hide that horse tattoo on her neck – a sure giveaway once the inevitable notice of her escape arrives from Athens.

Already Thratta is eyeing merchant caravans arriving from the north and wondering how to arrange passage with one of them on their return journey. She likes it here in southern Anatolia, but she yearns for the open plains of her homeland and the sight of the snow-capped Haemus Mountains lining the horizon to the north.

The Sprinter

After a brisk jog from the amphitheatre, Symilos the sprinter sits in the shade of a sacred grove and contemplates the massive, ridged trunk of an ancient plane tree. The tree is tall – twenty times the height of Symilos himself, and remarkably bushy. Here, under this same tree, the locals assure Symilos, Zeus romanced the nymph Europa after he had carried her from the Levant while in the form of a bull. King Minos was conceived on this very spot.

The story can be seen in two ways, the sprinter muses. On the one hand, we might consider it one of a couple eloping for a romantic interlude before the man has to return to his loveless marriage. On the other hand, we might view the taking of Europa as a violent abduction and this pleasant grove the spot where Zeus repeatedly raped his helpless victim. So much of the story depends on the teller.

As his contemplations over the duality of the story show, at present Symilos is somewhat ambivalent about

CLASSICAL CRETE

Crete was seen in many ways as being more Greek than mainland Greece. Many Greek customs and laws originated in Crete, which was also considered the birthplace of Zeus, king of the gods. In the Hellenistic era, a number of city-states rose to prominence, chief of these being Gortyn on the southern coast. Though the island was well positioned to benefit from trade between Egypt, Greece and Asia Minor, constant wars between the rival aristocracies of the city-states led to widespread poverty among the peasantry. Many Cretans hired themselves out as mercenaries – Cretan archers were in high demand – and it was not unusual to find Cretans on both sides of any contemporary conflict. Other Cretans packed up and moved to more peaceful locations in Greece and Asia. Some dispossessed Cretans took to the sea and Cretan pirates became a menace to international trade until they were finally suppressed by the Romans in the first century BC, who eventually brought the entire island under their control.

Crete in general and Gortyn in particular. There can be no doubt that Gortyn is an impressive city. It has strong walls, a towering acropolis and some of the best stadium facilities that he has ever seen. There's also something of an edge to the mood of the bustling crowd that packs the agora in the mornings, a kind of restless energy and ambition – a determination to get ahead no matter what the cost to oneself or others.

This is all well and good, and indeed Symilos became an Olympic-class sprinter through having much the same attitude. But is it an atmosphere in which a man would want to spend the rest of his life? This is the question that he has come to ponder.

The visit to Crete began normally enough, though in retrospect the welcome given when Symilos and his entourage had disembarked at Gortyn's harbour of Lebena had been almost suspiciously effusive. The sprinter, his trainer and masseur were set up in a rented house not far from the amphitheatre, where attentive servants awaited their every command. True, Symilos was the star sprinter at the premier event of the coming athletic festival, but even with this consideration, the city authorities had been exceptionally oleaginous. Frankly, the stream of ornate compliments and insincere flattery had begun to grate on Symilos' nerves.

The games he was here to compete in had followed the pattern familiar from dozens of similar events across the Hellenistic world. First there had been a procession to the stadium and sacrifices to the honour of Athena, the city's patron deity. Then speeches, since the city was currently a democracy and no politician facing re-election will miss a chance to put himself before the voters. On the next day the actual events had begun. A large audience had turned out for the games, not only because their attendance honoured the goddess but also because excellence at athletics and appreciation of athletes is one of the defining characteristics of a Hellene, and the Cretans regard themselves as being even more Hellenic than the folk in Greece itself.

The first day's contests included the long jump, discus and javelin, and day two the brutal boxing, the wrestling and the *pankration*, which is something of a mixture between the two. Then followed the pentathlon, in which athletes demonstrated versatility by competing in five of the major events, and an entire day was given over to chariot-racing, in which Cretan aristocrats tried strenuously to outdo each other with both the speed and the magnificence of their chariots and horses.

Symilos noticed an ominous ferocity and bitterness in these aristocratic contests, a depth of rivalry that does not bode well for the political well-being of the island. Factional fighting, often escalating to full-blown civil wars, are the curse of Greek civic life. Often one well-established family will take a demagogic line, claiming the support of the people against an over-mighty establishment (and their own political rivals). At which all the 'best people' (which is what *aristoi* means in Greek) will fall in behind an opposing leader from among their own and, well, things go downhill from there.

Usually, Symilos pays such matters little attention. There's usually a truce for religious festivals even between cities at war, and so he can come in, run his race and quickly depart for more salubrious climes – hopefully bearing a victor's spoils. Yet Gortyn is different.

The *stadion*, the final sprint, was the climactic event of the festival. The track was wide and smooth, Symilos was still in peak form after his Alexandrian victory and he won so easily that he was actually able to stop at the finish line and watch the competition for second and third place develop behind him.

Then, that same evening, to celebrate his victory Symilos was invited to dinner by one of the city's top politicians at his home on the slopes of the acropolis. It was an intimate affair and afterwards sprinter and host sat together on a balcony looking south to where the distant Mediterranean glinted in the moonlight. Both men spilled wine as a libation to the gods and then the politician made his pitch.

Essentially it was this: Gortyn would pay a fortune for Symilos to abandon his Neapolitan citizenship and instead take up residence in the Cretan city. The runner would then be ceremonially enrolled in the Gortyn city register as a citizen in good standing and compete in the coming Olympics as 'Symilos of Gortyn'.

It's a tempting offer, and the politician was very persuasive. Instead of being exiled from his native city by the ongoing war between Rome and Carthage, Symilos can return 'home' whenever he likes. There he can make full use of Gortyn's extensive athletics training facilities rather than being dependent on the goodwill of patrons to supply these. Furthermore, Symilos will be transferring from a city at the edges of the Greek world to one right in the Hellenic heartland. Travel to athletic events will be easier and between these festivals Symilos will no longer be a peripatetic wanderer.

The politician pointed out that long gone are the days when it was almost impossible for a Greek to transfer his allegiance from one city to another. Over the past decades, the cities on the Greek mainland have been relentlessly emptied by an outflow of citizens leaving their birthplace to take up residence in the newly founded Greek cities of Asia Minor, Egypt and the Levant. Such citizens are actively recruited by the leaders of the new cities, even as Symilos was now being recruited.

Why scratch a living from the poor soil of Greece when there are fertile farms to be had on the banks of the Nile or alongside the Tigris? Likewise, why should Symilos keep citizenship in the city from which he has been so long cut off? Just as Alexander's conquests have opened up a new world for Hellenistic emigrants, why should the athletic prowess of Symilos not allow him to upgrade his citizenship to that of a better-placed city?

So now Symilos sits in the sacred grove and ponders his options. Gortyn would welcome him with open arms, but the city of his birth would see only an opportunistic betrayal. The plaques in his honour would be torn down, his very existence expunged from the city records. How would history see Symilos should he accept Gortyn's offer and then go on to triumph at the Olympics? Will he be remembered as a cynical turncoat or as a pragmatic athlete? Or, as with the story of Zeus and Europa, will it depend on who is doing the telling?

4

ΜΑΧΑΝΕΥΣ
ΠΡΟΕΤΟΙΜΑΣΙΕΣ

(January – Preparations)

The Bride

Pamphilius is the only son of a wealthy shipbuilder. He is of a good family, single and extremely good-looking – chiselled chin, flaxen hair and blue eyes. He is also a womanizer who habituates brothels and keeps company with street prostitutes. He is overly fond of wine and can get vicious when drunk. In fact, so nasty can Pamphilius become after several cups of wine that his first wife petitioned the city archons for a divorce. It is rare for Greek women to divorce their husbands and the wife's reputation seldom survives the scandal. The woman has to present her petition in person – one of the few times when a woman can represent herself in court – and in this case her swollen lip and black eye certainly made her argument more persuasive. That and Pamphilius' ripe reputation made the divorce a formality.

Now Pamphilius is in search of a new wife, and to this end he has sounded out Appia's parents, offering to give the family an interest-free loan for the dowry that her parents can't afford and vowing that later he will discreetly forgive the loan. In effect, then, he will be paying his new wife's dowry to himself. In a sane world, Apphia reflects, there would be no need to go through such convoluted and pointless financial dealings. But this is Athens, and the size of a dowry reflects prestige on both parties in the transaction. Should Apphia be 'given away' for free, the reputation of her father and her new husband would suffer alike.

In the event, it looks as though the question may be purely academic. Apphia's parents were initially impressed by the good looks and family connections of their daughter's suitor and relieved to find a way out of the predicament of finding her a dowry of a respectable size. Apphia's sisters were less impressed; frankly, they were horrified. In Athens, women may not get out of the house much but when they do, they get together to gossip. It did not take intensive investigation by the sisters to turn up abundant evidence to prove that far from being a changed man – as Pamphilius had earnestly alleged – he has continued in his old ways, exactly as before. Apphia's parents are keen to marry off their daughter but they are also genuinely concerned for her welfare. Very much to their daughters' relief, negotiations for the nuptials have been called off while the parents wait for a better offer.

WIVES IN ANCIENT GREECE

In some Greek cities, a bride wore a crown of asparagus – a warning to the groom that the sweet part of the plant was protected by thorns. This ambivalence nicely sums up the role of a Greek wife. As the person who managed household affairs, she certainly had the capacity to make her husband's life miserable if she chose but, ultimately, she was completely subordinate to him. (In his *Lysistrata*, playwright Aristophanes takes it for granted that husbands routinely spanked their wives.) It did not help the woman's situation that a bride might be half her husband's age, for women were meant to be married soon after menarche, usually between fifteen and eighteen, and men usually married at age thirty. And while the house was a woman's domain, she was not expected to venture out much, and when she did she was heavily veiled and cloaked.

Yet whatever Pamphilius' failings as a human being, at least he lives locally. Ever since his suit was put on hold, Apphia's mother has been getting lyrical about the beauty and general desirability of their ancestral homeland of Elis. As is the case with most girls of her class, Apphia's education has been a somewhat hit-and-miss affair. She is, of course, a practised if not particularly skilled weaver, and she can read, write and do arithmetic to the extent needed to handle household accounts. Yet no one has bothered to teach her geography and all Apphia knows of Elis is that the place her family came from is far, far away, and that occasionally strangers from that distant city-state stay as guests at their house.

Now that the house has another Elean guest, Apphia's mother is suspiciously eager to tell her daughter all about her family's origins. Apparently, Elis is ancient – its people are mentioned in the epics of Homer – and peaceful, for the city-state has managed to pick the right side in all of the major political upheavals that have troubled Greece over the past few centuries.

Nor is Elis actually that far away, it seems. A quick trip to Corinth is followed by a cruise across the Gulf of Corinth, which takes one to the Ionian Sea, and then one is already practically at Elis. Really it's so straightforward that their visitor did the trip in ten days despite the inclement winter weather. The city itself is splendid, with a huge agora surrounded by temples. The temple to Aphrodite has an impressive statue of the goddess formed from gold and

A FAMILY SCENE

ivory and there's an equally awesome temple to Apollo on the other side of the market. There's a large hippodrome, a theatre rivalling even the theatre of Dionysus in Athens and, in short, all the accoutrements of civilization.

It's not hard to see where Apphia's mother is going with this so Apphia has taken several long, thoughtful looks at the Elean guest-friend (*Xenos*) who is staying with them. As expected, the man is far too well mannered to visit or even to stare too long at the *gynaikeia*, the women's quarters, but Apphia has seen him entering and leaving the house on several occasions. The man is no Apollo, that's certain. He is short, dark and rather plump with a slightly nervous, fussy manner and he probably has damp palms.

Yet none of this is a particularly crippling disadvantage, for Apphia's sisters assure her that in a marriage good looks wear off quickly. What a wife needs most from a husband is firstly a considerate nature, secondly generosity with the household budget and thirdly an occupation that keeps him out of the house most of the time. Yes, Apphia replies plaintively, but what if she can't understand a word that her spouse is saying?

This is indeed something of a snag, for the folk of Elis are notorious *phonobarbari* – that is, while their city might cleave to the finest tenets of Hellenic civilization, their spoken Greek bears little resemblance to the mellifluous tones of the average Athenian and quite a strong resemblance to the guttural grunts of Romans, Illyrians and other barbarians. It's not just that the Eleans are Dorians, for most peoples of the Peloponnese are members of that Greek tribe. And while the Dorian dialect is markedly different

81

from the Athenian Ionic, Spartans, for example, though immediately recognizable by their broad vowels and flattened consonants are – unlike the Eleans – at least comprehensible to the untrained ear.

Apphia will never admit it to her parents but she has on occasion sneaked downstairs to listen to their guest in conversation with her father. Her father sometimes has reason to travel to Elis on family business, but it is clear that, despite being more accustomed to the accent, even he struggles at times to grasp the meaning hidden in his guest's braying utterances. The thought that she might one day raise children who speak with the same barbaric tones is one that Apphia can barely bring herself to contemplate. Even assuming that, despite her exile from Athens, she and her sisters sometimes meet for family occasions, how will she cope with the mortification of her kinsfolk hearing her children speak?

Yet these appear to be the choices – to live in Athens with the brute Pamphilius or to live far from friends and family in alien, and literally incomprehensible, Elis. Truly it is an accursed thing to be a fourth daughter and doubly accursed when even in the face of two such invidious choices it is not even she but her parents who get to choose.

〰〰〰〰〰〰〰〰〰〰〰〰〰〰〰〰〰〰〰〰〰〰〰〰

The Builder

With bargaining for the use of his oxen complete, the peasant-farmer leaves Meton's office and the architect lays his head gently upon his work-desk. Nine months! It is ridiculous – certainly nine months is plenty of time for a baby to go from conception to birth, or for Persephone to spend in the upper world before she rejoins her husband in Hades – but no one has ever built a temple in nine months. Take the temple of Olympian Zeus, started in Athens two-and-a half centuries ago [in 520 BC]. Construction has been going at a steady pace, interrupted by the occasional war or plague, and the builders confidently expect to have the place operational within the next 200 years, give or take a century or two. That's how you build a temple.

Yet Ptolemy's envoy had been adamant: if the new temple of Serapis is not receiving worshippers before the next Olympics, then the Egyptian was not interested in having the thing built at all. So, assuming that cost is no object, can Meton build the temple in that time? Logically, the short answer is 'no', and that is the reason why several rival builders turned down the commission immediately, for the canny Egyptians have insisted on contractual obligations so severe that any builder whose temple is constructed after the impossibly tight deadline will end up paying for the thing himself.

There's a story about Charos of Lindos that troubles Meton's dreams. Charos was a famous builder who was commissioned by the people of Rhodes to build the colossal statue that is now one of the wonders of the world. Originally the design was for something 50 cubits high (23 metres, or 75 feet) – massive and monumental, but not unheard of. Then the people of Rhodes asked Charos whether he could build something twice as high, thus turning a monumental statue into something that would amaze the peoples of the entire known world. Naturally Charos had agreed and, as an afterthought, added that, since he was doubling the height of the statue, he would need to double his fee.

The problem was that the material-to-height ratio of such statues is exponential and not linear – so Charos ended up needing to pay for eight times the amount of material he would have needed for a 50-cubit statue. The project was recently finished by another builder, for the bankrupt and humiliated Charos committed suicide before construction was complete.

The tale might be apocryphal, but the moral is real, and no other builder but Meton was prepared to take the considerable risks that a high-speed temple might involve. And Meton was only prepared to take that risk because he has been working around Olympia for some time and extensive local knowledge gives him a hidden extra advantage. For example, he knows that there's a promontory of Mount Skaphídi, not far from the small city of Pheia, where the people of the city had once erected a temple to Poseidon, god of the sea.

For some reason, the temple was not pleasing to the son of Kronos, and barely had construction been completed (after a leisurely decade of building work) than the earth-shaking god destroyed it in an eyeblink with a brief but violent earth tremor that left the rest of the city almost totally undamaged. The people of Pheia could take a hint and had not attempted to repair the temple – especially as the quake had wrecked it so comprehensively that an almost total rebuild would be needed. Thereafter, unwanted by the god for whom it had been built, the remains of the temple had lain mouldering in the grass for decades.

This snippet of local knowledge had occurred to Meton after he had regretfully rejected the Egyptian's demands as being simply impossible. Once Meton did remember about the ruined temple he had immediately hurried to the site to assess its potential. Fortunately, Pheia is the port city for Olympia and Ptolemy's representative was already in town as he prepared to embark for home. Meton was able to intercept the envoy and make his pitch for repositioning and reconstructing the ruined building as a new temple for Serapis.

Given that his mission would otherwise be a failure, Ptolemy's agent was certainly ready to consider the plan. But, given that Poseidon is a jealous god with a penchant for wholesale destruction, nothing would go ahead unless it was clear that the deity had no objection to his abandoned temple being removed and reoccupied by a divine newcomer.

Poseidon is not well represented in Elis, which mainly dedicates its worship to Zeus, the city's patron god, and to Hera, his wife. There is, however, a splendid temple to the sea god at Tainaron, a peninsula in the south Peloponnese. To there, Meton and the Ptolemaic agent sent a messenger outlining their plans and asking whether their proposal would be acceptable to the god.

The cynical builder was unsurprised to discover that Poseidon would be happy to release the material of his former temple in exchange for some highly expensive ritual dedications in his name. A further, equally expensive payment by the Egyptians calmed any religious qualms of the Elean priesthood and council, though the council has 500 members, and Meton still wonders how much it cost to bring each member around. One thing he does know – all this took time to arrange and time is the one thing the Egyptians can't give him.

Fortunately, the cost of dressed stone being what it is, it is not unusual for ruins to be used as a source of material for new buildings, so what Meton is proposing is by no means revolutionary. For example, after much of the sacred Athenian Acropolis was destroyed in the Persian wars, the Athenians used the rubble as construction material for their new and grander design and repurposed the surviving buildings to fit the scheme. So Meton has precedent on his side, a commission from the Egyptians and a temple for the god to occupy at Olympia, albeit one currently in the wrong place in a state of disassembly and literal dilapidation. So now Meton has merely to get the temple transported to Olympia and reassembled in record time.

Unsurprisingly, given that the region is occupied by Greeks of the Dorian tribe, the architecture of the temple was of the Doric order. Where once Meton had wanted the Doric style for reasons of economy, now he is glad that the former temple is of the simpler style because in a Doric temple there is less to get damaged and what is damaged will be easier to repair.

For example, a Doric column capital is a plain cylinder of stone that performs the basic task of supporting the

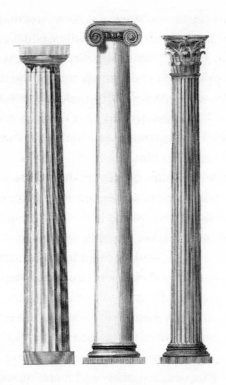

GREEK TEMPLE COLUMNS – FROM LEFT TO RIGHT,
DORIC (FLUTED), IONIC AND CORINTHIAN

square beam of the architrave on the roof. Any damage
to the column or the capital can be easily remedied by the
judicious addition of marble dust mixed with concrete,
especially as the columns will be painted over anyway.
Now, had that column capital been of the Corinthian
order, there would have been a sort of flowery explosion
of carved stone leaves at the top, any one of which could
have broken off when the column toppled, necessitating
expensive and time-consuming repairs.

Another advantage helping with the rebuilding of the temple is that those in the Hellenistic world tend to arrive in kit form anyway. That is, entire sections of the temple are usually constructed near the quarry from which the stone is extracted. After all, when one is sending blocks of stone substantial distances, it is only sensible to ensure that they are all going to fit together on arrival at the other end.

So, for example, the columns of a temple peristyle (a roofed colonnade surrounding a space) come in the form of drums of stone that are to be mounted one on top of the other to make the completed columns. Each drum comes with identifying marks chiselled into the stone somewhere that will not be visible after final assembly. These marks denote, say, the first drum of the outermost left-hand column, after which it is a matter of Meton hunting through the ruins to find where the second drum of the left-hand column rolled off to, and so on. The base upon which the temple sits is completely intact and this really only needs excavating, after which the blocks of stone will be painfully transported by wagon, one by one until they are reseated in the new foundations, which Meton's engineers are already digging out at Olympia.

From Pheia to Olympia is a distance of some 210 *stades* (40 km or 25 miles), and almost every part of the temple will need repair and reconstruction before the eventual rededication. This series of challenges must be completed within nine months – a proposition that, given sufficient manpower and unlimited funds, can be done. All Meton has to do is make sure that it *is* done – for he now stands to lose his reputation and retirement prospects should he fail.

The Merchant

Alexandria may be in Egypt, but it is a Greek city through and through (though there's a large and growing Jewish population who might disagree). It's a young city, for it was founded by Alexander the Great around a century ago. He never saw what his city was to become because, immediately after ordering the foundation, the conquering general set off once more on his travels and eventually died in Babylon, far to the east.

Yet if Alexander never saw Alexandria again, Alexandria certainly saw Alexander – and continues to do so on a daily basis. Once he had died, Alexander's body was sent to his Macedonian home for burial in state – but it never arrived. Instead, the father of Ptolemy II (who could be just as annoying as his son) hijacked the funeral train and took the body to Egypt where it now lies preserved as both a tourist attraction and a clear reminder that Ptolemaic Egypt is heir to the Macedonian Hellenistic tradition.

For the merchant Sakion, the mortal remains of Alexander are far less significant than the remains that Alexander left elsewhere – namely all over the city of Tyre on the coast of the Levant. Tyre had the impudence to attempt to withstand Alexander's armies and, being largely surrounded by water, proved exceedingly difficult to capture. Yet captured it was, and Alexander took out on Tyre his extreme frustration at having had his career of conquest delayed by almost a year.

Before Alexander reduced it to smoking rubble and corpses, proud Tyre had once been the major trading port of Mediterranean civilization, the place where goods from the East met demand from the West. With Tyre as devastated economically as it had been in every other way, merchants from across two continents looked for another trading centre to take up the slack. And Alexandria was perfectly positioned to do the job – in fact, given the city's easy access to trade goods arriving via the Red Sea, Alexandria was even better suited as a hub for international trade than Tyre had been.

As well as Tyre, Alexandria has replaced another city. For centuries, Greece had traded goods and ideas with Egypt through the port of Naucratis, a coastal city that was half Greek and half Egyptian in character. Now Naucratis is in steep decline, both because the silting of the Canopic branch of the Nile has restricted navigation to the port and because Alexandria has sucked away all the best and most ambitious Greek traders – including the merchant Sakion and his family.

Another advantage of Alexandria is that it is a planned city rather than an ancient foundation that grew higgledy-piggledy from some disorganized primeval village. The Greeks are remarkably good at city planning (though some ancient cities in Anatolia give the lie to their claim that they invented the science) and one result of careful planning is that the streets of the city are cleverly angled to pick up the cooling breezes that blow in from the sea across the harbour at Pharos.

Lying in his rooftop garden, Sakion very much

appreciates these breezes, for he has been out of sorts ever since his return downriver from Edfu. On returning to Alexandria a fortnight ago, he had hosted a small symposium to celebrate his return to (Hellenic) civilization – and this was not some arty philosophical gathering but a proper symposium, the name of which derives from the words meaning 'drinking together'. Sakion and friends indeed drunk together well into the night, and the hangover with which Sakion had awakened the next morning has been stubbornly difficult to shake.

At least Sakion does not have to travel to Pergamon to offload his ivory. Almost as soon as his barge docked at the river port of Lake Mareotis, the Egyptian religious authorities requisitioned the entire cargo (for very handsome recompense). Some of the ivory will be used in the new Serapeum, which Ptolemy is building for his god in Alexandria, and Sakion has been commissioned to transport the rest to Greece where another temple to Serapis is under construction at Olympia.

Apparently, the Greek temple is not yet ready, so Sakion has spent the past few days arranging for the storage of his (or rather now, the state's) ivory. Ivory is organic material, and one cannot just leave it piled up in a warehouse somewhere. While it is pretty much impervious to insects, direct sunlight can bleach the ivory to an unpleasant pale yellow. Even more important, given the Alexandrian climate and its extremes of heat and humidity, is the fact that ivory is hygroscopic. This means that in humid conditions the tusks will absorb water like a set of curved white sponges, swelling and warping in the process. Then, as the air gets less humid – say on a chilly desert night – the ivory gives up that moisture, but unevenly, so that splits and cracks develop across the surface, ruining the quality of the material.

It took some time, but eventually Sakion found ideal storage for the tusks in the *naos* of a temple to Demeter on the outskirts of the city. There's a modest ivory statue of Demeter in that central room, and because votive offerings to the goddess are stored there also, the room is secure. A large open krater of water keeps the humidity constant and the attendants who regularly rub down the statue with a mixture of olive and almond oil have agreed to do the same with Sakion's tusks. The ivory will keep safely until Sakion can transport it across the Mediterranean in midsummer.

Not that Sakion plans to remain idle until then – he is already busily making plans to fill the remaining winter months. A contact in Bactria has sent a message that he is looking for an end buyer for a large shipment of silk, which is already on the move from a way station near Arbela in the eastern Seleucid empire [in modern Kurdistan]. This will do nicely to placate those rather annoyed merchants in Pergamon to whom Sakion had promised the ivory that the Egyptian authorities have requisitioned.

Given unsettled conditions in Mesopotamia, the merchants in Arbela plan to ship the silk down the River Tigris and then across the chain of oases in the Syrian desert to Palmyra. Sakion will himself pick up the cargo at Sidon and stay with a colleague until the sea routes reopen with the spring, then accompany the goods to Pergamon, renewing personal contacts along the way.

Pergamon is a seaport on the River Caicus, right on the coast, yet with much of the city hundreds of metres higher on the terraced mesa that overlooks the harbour. It's about as healthy a city as can be found anywhere in the world, and the ideal place for Sakion to recover from whatever malaise he has picked up in southern Egypt.

The Lyre Player

Kallia sits herself on a marble bench in the garden and carefully unwraps her *kithara*. There's this much to be said for a lyre, even a top-rate lyre such as her *kithara*: unlike some more bulky musical instruments, one can take a lyre almost anywhere and play it upon arrival. This does not mean that all conditions are equally suitable for a musical performance, though, and at present Kallia wants to ensure that the damp sea air blowing in from the harbour is not having a damaging effect on the lyre's strings. The body of the lyre has been lightly oiled to prevent moisture being absorbed by the wood but the strings are a fine mix of ox gut and thin wire, and there's no way to prevent the organic part from soaking up humidity from the air.

This is not a serious issue, however, provided that the tuning of the harp is amended to take account of the circumstances, and tuning the lyre is one of the things that Kallia has come into here to do. The garden is well suited to music, being beautiful and, like many urban gardens in Pergamon, a fine mix of functionality and aesthetics. The

PROFESSIONAL LYRE PLAYER WITH A *KITHARA*

trees that bend over the bench are pear and pomegranate, with a fine little apple tree growing in a large pot in the corner of the courtyard. In summer, these trees provide shade, but also fruit, and the pond watered by a small ornamental fountain contains a substantial population of carp, which both keep the bugs down and regularly grace the table at dinner.

Kallia has already tried the carp, and it is delicious, for the sort of person who can afford to keep an in-house lyre player is also the sort of person who can afford a top-rate chef. Naturally, Kallia does not dine at the same time as her host, for not only would it be inappropriate for her to do so with the men but Kallia is also there to provide a musical accompaniment to the meal.

When there's a symposium, Kallia kicks things off with a *spondeion*, a tune of tongue-in-cheek solemnity that accompanies the ritual libations in which wine is spilled in veneration of the gods whom the participants at the symposium have chosen to honour. Since Kallia's patron is a wealthy merchant, that divinity is usually Hermes, god of merchants and con men (when the two are not the same).

Another reason for her visit to the garden is to work on a personalized *spondeion*. The new song is Kallia's own composition, and since she suspects that she will be singing it a lot, she has chosen a well-known melody and made the song a riff on the Orphic hymn to Hermes. Her patron is planning an important dinner with some well-connected colleagues next month and she wants to be pitch-perfect before then.

Not only will Kallia perform at symposia, but also at more elevated musical affairs where she will be expected to reproduce the finest lyrical compositions of such musicians as Pindar, Lasus of Hermione and Simonides of Ceos.

As she plucks the strings with practised fingers, Kallia sometimes stops to fiddle with the pegs at the top of the lyre. Tightening a string produces a higher pitch, loosening takes it down a tone or two – but not more, because the metal-to-ox-gut ratio of the strings is tailored for their expected range, with the higher notes being more metallic.

To some extent, Kallia agrees with Pythagoras, that same philosopher who discovered that in a triangle the square of the hypotenuse is equal to the sum of the square of the other two sides. (Who needs to know that? Kallia wonders.) Of much greater importance is that other discovery of Pythagoras: that the frequency of a vibrating lyre string is in inverse proportion to its length. Where Pythagoras and Kallia fall out in musical theory is that Pythagoras maintains that music is a function of mathematics and he has arranged his musical scales as a stack of perfect fifths.

Perhaps this works in the towns of southern Italy where Pythagoras did his musical theorizing, but again, unlike Pythagoras, Kallia knows from experience that music has an *ethnos* – a tribal culture. Because Pythagoras believed that music is the acoustic expression of mathematics, it follows that perfect music should be pleasing to all people – just as are the symmetry of a butterfly's wings or the petals of a flower. Yet Kallia knows that this is just not so – for example, the Galatians like fast, melody-driven tunes with which they can sing along (unsurprising, since '*melodia*' in Greek means 'sing' or 'chant'), while the Greeks of Ionia prefer lyrical compositions in which the underlying tune is based upon the poetic verses of the song. An Ionian who attempts to sing along with a top performer is likely to get something heavy hurled at him. The musical theorist Aristoxenus has actually composed a set of musical scales suited best for each *ethnos*, including the rich notes of the Lydian, the wilder, less structured Phrygian and the spare, clear notes of the Dorian.

By and large, Kallia agrees with Aristoxenus and feels that rather than setting her scales from highest to lowest note at mathematical intervals, the tuning of her lyre should be done partly by feel and trained intuition. A human has five senses of sight, smell, touch, hearing and taste, and a lyre has 'senses' of note, interval, tone and pitch, and just as a human might have keen eyesight but poor hearing, an individual lyre string might have good tone but weaker pitch, and the tuning must be adapted to take account of these relative strengths and weaknesses.

Just to complicate things further, Kallia might also need to retune her lyre depending on the occasion. She has already been contacted by the Pergamene city authorities, who have no intention of letting her merchant patron keep a world-class musician to himself. Kallia has already been contracted to play in the religious processions that are a regular feature of any Greek city's civic life, and the *prosodion* she will be playing on these occasions need to have the sounds of her lyre working in harmony with the flutes and percussion instruments both in the procession and at the events afterwards.

It occurs to Kallia that there are almost no parts of Greek life that are not usually accompanied by music. In fact, as Aristotle once discussed, music may be so much a part of life that we listen all the while unaware: 'The movement of the stars produces a harmony ... which is in our ears from the moment of birth and is thus for us indistinguishable from silence, just as coppersmiths are so accustomed to the sounds of the smithy that they no longer hear them.'

It's an appealing theory – that all things alive are surrounded by music – and what Kallia does while plucking her strings in the garden is to pick out themes from that music and, by amplifying and separating them, she makes them again audible to the human ear.

5

ΔΩΔΕΚΑΤΕΥΣ ΠΡΩΤΑ ΒΗΜΑΤΑ

(February – First Steps)

@@@@@@@@@@@@@@@@@@@@@@@@@@@@@@@

The Farmer

There's a north wind blowing, and the bitter feel of frost in the air. Iphita is preparing to leave the heat of her fireside to check on the grain bins at the back of the barn. In this cold weather, the oxen will eat more and Iphita has to carefully balance the food supply for her livestock with the grain available to her farmworkers. She needs both men and animals for the spring, but while icy Boreas – the god of the north wind – sends his freezing gusts down the side of Mount Kronos, all that any living thing can do is hunker down and wait for things to get better. And though useless for now, the beasts keep eating, as do the men who hang around the fire in the blacksmith's smithy exchanging gossip when they should be checking and oiling harnesses and ensuring that everything is ready for the hard work to come with the spring.

Iphita sighs and prepares to leave the snug warmth of the farmhouse. With advancing age, she feels more keenly the pangs of rheumatism that have troubled her from childhood, and she makes a note to pick up more willow-bark potion from the herbalist when the market next sets up in the village.

For now, she armours herself against the weather by selecting a soft coat of lambswool, one that she made for herself when younger, weaving thick wool with thin warp for tight-packed, wind-resistant threads. Feet that in summer she thrusts carelessly into sandals are now carefully laced into felt-lined oxhide boots, while her hair is neatly tucked under a weatherproof felt cap precisely shaped to accommodate her coiled tresses.

The farmer ruefully examines the heavy black clouds scudding across the morning sky and pauses at the door to unhook a kid-skin cloak stitched with ox sinew and greased with goose fat on the outside. Thus warmed and waterproofed against anything but a full-scale downpour, Iphita steps outside.

This is the hardest month, when the crop is struggling to establish itself in the field and the starving deer sneak from the woods to demolish the young shoots before the late-coming dawn. Even the hens are producing fewer eggs and the dugs of the newly pregnant nanny-goats have not yet swelled with milk. Every nightfall, Iphita squints at the evening sky, eager for the first glimpse of Arcturus above the horizon, for the rising of that star signals that the worst of winter has passed, and with that first hint of spring it will be time to trim the fruit trees in the orchard and prune the vines. Should she leave the pruning until the return of the first swallows, the vines will have wasted valuable resources on new shoots in branches that will be cut away.

Returning from the feed bins, Iphita notices a stir of activity at the Olympic precinct. It's early in the year for preparations to begin for the forthcoming Games, though work on that temple to some newfangled Egyptian god has been going on annoyingly and noisily in all but the worst of the winter weather. Nothing awaits Iphita at home but household tasks, some tedious weaving and repairs to some faded work clothes, so she readily indulges her curiosity and wanders over to the precinct to see what is going on.

It's something serious, certainly, because Iphita can see the coloured cloaks of aristocrats and hear the chanting of priests. There is also a mass of workmen who are busily levering something up the path towards the temple of Hera, about which most of the activity is concentrated. The ox-carts that delivered the material wait patiently outside the gates of the precinct, the drivers giving their beasts a rest before they take the muddy, potholed road back to town. (Greek roads are generally intended for foot-traffic only and it is not unusual for wheeled vehicles to struggle on even well-used thoroughfares.)

Iphita goes to strike up a conversation with one of the drivers. While the convention restricting women from the sacred precinct is only strictly enforced during the Games,

EXAMPLE OF A DORIC TEMPLE OF HERA (FROM PAESTUM, ITALY)

it might be more diplomatic for Iphita to remain outside on this occasion – though the irony is not lost on her that one of the main temples in the precinct where women are not normally allowed is that same temple of Hera, a goddess who is quite certainly female, and the wife of mighty Zeus himself. Furthermore, every four years the statue of the goddess in her temple is dressed in fresh robes woven for her by the women of Elis. These robes are made of flax, for it is a sign of the favour of the goddess that flax grows in Elis and nowhere else on the Greek mainland.

Women, unsurprisingly, are not allowed to participate in the Olympics, but then the men of Elis are strongly discouraged from watching the events of the Heraia. This is the women-only games that usually take place two years before the androcentric main event of the Olympics and the one time when women occupy the precinct. Iphita has never been a competitor at the Games, for her sturdy frame is hardly suited for running and the events are all footraces in which the girls – virgins all – compete with their hair unbound and clad in only a scandalously short tunic. Iphita has still taken part in the Games though, for as a local and well-respected landowner, she has been among the panel of judges who adjudicate the suitability of candidates for the races and the results afterwards.

The problem with being a judge at these events is that one is expected to participate in the ceremonial choral dances sacred to the founders of the athletic event – Hippodamia, the wife of that Pelops after whom the Peloponnese is named, and Physkoa, a local woman beloved of the wine god Dionysus. Iphita is embarrassingly lacking in the grace needed for the proper performance of these dances and feels that one of the few benefits of widowhood is that these days she need not participate – for the judges must be married women.

Women can enter the sacred precinct during the Heraia because the temple of Hera is central to the event. No one knows for certain when the temple was built but it is certainly very old – older, in fact, than the Olympics. There are two clear indications of this – firstly the statue of Hera is of a crude ancient style (known as an *agalma*), and that shows the queen of the gods seated on her throne while her husband, helmeted and bearded, stands beside her. Secondly, the pillars used to support the temple architrave are of wood, rather than the stone columns that have been the norm in recent centuries. These wood pillars are clearly ancient, and the weathered trunks so warped and split that strategically placed metal bands must be secured around the pillars so that they can continue to do their work.

Of course, despite the care lavished on the pillars, if damp gets into a crack, the wood rots from the inside and eventually there is no option but to replace the pillar with one of stone. In the nine centuries or so that the temple has stood here, almost two-thirds of the pillars have so been replaced, with the mismatched replacement pillars themselves a testament to changes in architectural styles through the ages.

So now another pillar is being replaced – and with great ceremony, for such an event occurs but once or twice in a century. All this Iphita ascertains though her conversation with the ox-cart driver, for the man is bored with waiting and happy to pass the time. Iphita has chores waiting at the farmhouse, however, and so says her farewell, making a note to sneak in later and see how the renovations have turned out.

The Diplomat

It is not often that one spends the afternoon in the company of a god, and once back in his chambers, Persaeus orders a servant to bring him a beaker of wine while he considers the experience. For a start, gods are probably meant to look more, well … divine. True, there have been occasions when even mighty Zeus has disguised himself as a mortal for his own devious purposes (usually involving the seduction of some unfortunate princess), but if this is the case with Antiochus II Theos, king of the Seleucid empire, then it is an incredibly effective disguise.

The man (or god) whom the Macedonian envoy had met was a somewhat slightly-built fellow in his late thirties, who had a large nose, deep-set eyes and the expression of a pet hound unfairly denied an expected treat. King Antiochus' prematurely greying hair was arranged in an elaborate coiffure over a silken band that singularly failed to disguise a growing bald spot. Despite its tonsorial failings, this silk band is of considerable significance, for it is of the type called a 'diadem' and it signifies that the wearer is of extraordinary importance, even among his fellow monarchs.

This is certainly the case with Antiochus (whom Persaeus has to make a mental effort to avoid referring to as 'young Antiochus', both because he knew the man's father and because the monarch whom he himself serves – Antigonus Gonatus of Macedon – is twice the age of the Seleucid king). Despite his relative youth, Antiochus is monarch of one of the largest kingdoms the world has ever seen – or he will be, should he succeed in regaining control of the rebel satrapies of Parthia and Bactria, which have for the moment opted to go their own way under new management.

One may wonder how the man who has managed to lose around 40 per cent of his father's empire nevertheless qualifies as a god, but for this Antiochus has to thank the people of Miletus. Miletus is a Hellenistic city that sits at the mouth of the famously meandering River Meander in

Anatolia. During the recent war fought between Ptolemy II of Egypt and the Seleucids, city-states such as Miletus were important factors in the struggle for control of the Aegean Sea. At the time, Miletus was ruled by a tyrant – which in the Hellenistic world merely signifies a ruler who has come to power through unorthodox means and is supported by the military. But in this case the tyrant truly was tyrannical and the people of Miletus were deeply relieved when he was ejected from power by Antiochus, even though Antiochus had done the deed not out of altruism but because the tyrant had been a supporter of his enemy Ptolemy.

Because Miletus was far from his kingdom's Syrian heartlands, Antiochus lacked the military strength to take over rulership of the city, so he allowed the people to set up an independent government, which made the already delighted citizens deliriously happy. So happy were they that Antiochus was formally declared a god incarnate, and temples and sacred games were promised to his memory. Antiochus was rather pleased with the idea and has been trying to promote his worship elsewhere in his crumbling empire, albeit with very limited success.

Persaeus is very pleased that he has caught the divine Antiochus in his capital, for the king had only returned from campaign ten days before the diplomat's arrival. As a result, Persaeus has been quartered in very comfortable rooms in the city's citadel on Mount Silpius rather than having to bed down in an uncomfortable tent somewhere in a scorpion-infested desert. Less pleasing is the reason for the return of Antiochus to his capital – the king has received news that he is about to become a father once again.

The king already has three sons, but these are born of his former wife, the dispossessed and furious Laodice. Laodice had been put aside for the king's present wife, Berenice, daughter of Ptolemy II, a formidable lady whose irascible disposition is doubtless partly responsible for the king's permanent hangdog expression.

By treaty agreement with Ptolemy (a treaty that it is Persaeus' mission to break), if the child of Berenice is a boy, he will become the next ruler of the Seleucid empire, which will tilt the sympathies of that great empire towards Egypt and away from its current inclination towards Macedon. Indeed, one reason for the warm welcome that Persaeus has received from the Seleucid king is because the diplomat reminded the king of the empire's current connection to the Greek state as he arrived bearing gifts and letters from Antiochus' sister, who is married to Demetrios, the heir apparent of Macedon.

As he stands at the window, Persaeus takes an absent-minded swig of wine and from the heights of the citadel contemplates the barges moving far below along the River Orontes. It is unfortunate that diplomacy in the Hellenistic world is so tied up with the persons and personalities of the kings. A falling-out between brothers or the size of the dowry of a daughter can cause ructions in even the humblest of peasant families. Yet with the Hellenistic kings, these ructions lead not to a punch-up in a barnyard but to armies in motion and cities aflame.

Just to make it worse, treaties and alliances are made between these kings and not between the states they rule. So, for example, should Ptolemy II perish (and reports say that he has not been well lately) then every treaty and alliance that king has made becomes null and void and must be painfully renegotiated with his successor. When a Seleucid king dies, the heir must immediately rush around the separate bits of his far-flung empire and personally accept the obeisance of those of his predecessor's subjects who are prepared to give it. (The new king usually takes his army along on such occasions to make swearing fealty a persuasive option.)

Now and then, though, such personal relationships can produce dividends. Persaeus is rather looking forward to a meeting he has arranged for tomorrow with another envoy who has turned up to renew personal ties with the Seleucid king on behalf of the emperor of the fabled land of India.

Macedon does not have much to do with India, so this meeting is mainly for the two envoys to the Seleucid court to satisfy their mutual curiosity. Persaeus is keen to know more about that fabulous land of elephants and peacocks, a land so rich and populous that it was able to turn back even the invincible armies of Alexander the Great. In his turn, the Indian envoy wants to learn more about the strange and barbarous lands of the West and the complexities of Mediterranean culture.

Apparently, the Indian envoy's master is the emperor Asoka, a man who spent his early years in a blood-soaked campaign to unite the Indian subcontinent under his rule. Then, when he was close to succeeding in this ambition, Asoka allegedly became repulsed by bloodshed and slaughter and instead opted for the life of peace and harmony embodied in the Buddhist religion.

With all the fervour of a new convert, Asoka is keen on spreading his religion as far as he can and Persaeus is expecting to get an earful on the subject from Asoka's envoy. As far as Persaeus can make out, Buddhism is a religion without gods, and he is looking forward to seeing how well this idea goes down with Antiochus II – a man who would like his subjects to believe that he himself is a god.

The Runaway

That same sunset that marks the end of the day for the diplomat Persaeus has no such significance for the runaway slave Thratta. She is currently several hundred miles to the north-west between the cities of Mylasa and Herakleia, seated on a crude wooden bench and trying hard to sort through the mass of dried leaves and grasses in front of her. Before the sun has fully set, she must have sorted these plants by category and type and taken them to her teacher for approval. Then, by lamplight, she will work late into the evening grinding, boiling and mixing the various herbs and setting the concoctions aside for inspection before bedtime. It's finicky and demanding work and sometimes Thratta wonders if she laboured less hard when she was a slave back in Athens.

It's a pity she had to leave Halicarnassus. Thratta had liked the place and the freedom that came from being an adolescent street urchin, but she had always known that the city was merely a stopping point on her journey. She was going to leave before spring anyway but matters came to a head when she was involved in a friendly tussle with a boy of her own age and her cloak came loose to reveal the horse tattoo on her neck. Not just the boy but also several adult bystanders had seen the tattoo and Thratta had fled to the sound of their shouted questions, for tattoos are not usual among Greek boys – but very common among slaves, escaped and otherwise.

As it happened, the fishmonger's wife for whom Thratta did odd jobs had been in discussions with a fellow herbalist at the market where she secured her raw materials. This herbalist was an itinerant who worked the agoras of Greek cities up and down the coast of Asia Minor and she was in

HERBALISM IN ANTIQUITY

Medicine in Hellenistic Greece was a mixture of superstition, folk belief and scientific treatments based on careful empirical study. Of these different branches, none were more precise than herbalism, which was based on over a millennium of experimentation of the effects of various plants on the human metabolism, which ranged from mild relief from headache (willow bark) to rapid death (aconite). We know that herbs and spices from as far away as Java made their way west during the Hellenistic era, and it is quite probable that sweet wormwood was among these.

need of an apprentice, her previous student having found the work too demanding and run off.

Within three days Thratta had left town, once again female and this time allegedly the granddaughter of said herbalist, Eudoxia, a wizened old lady from Phrygia who has an apparently insatiable appetite for gossip and wine. She and Thratta are travelling with a caravan that had packed goods from the wild and exotic lands beyond Bactria and are now gradually selling off their silks and spices in the markets of Anatolia.

While on the road, the herbalist is responsible for dishing out potions for the care of mule-drivers and their mules alike, and she generally sends Thratta out on gathering expeditions as they travel, with instructions to seek out and harvest particular plants from specific locations along the way. (Thratta notes that she is often

MEDIC AT WORK

tasked with locating and picking the olive-green buds of the caper bush, which are employed by the herbalist herself as a hangover cure.)

Gathering herbs is not that easy, even when her teacher has carefully shown Thratta the type of plant she is to collect. Thratta must take precise note of where she gathered each plant and the prevailing conditions when she did so. For example, sometimes she can't go collecting at all because herbs should only be harvested on a sunny day, preferably from a hillside or meadow.

On one occasion, Thratta had returned rather pleased with herself because she had recognized the slim green leaves of rock samphire and picked an armful of it as well as the herbs she had been sent to gather. Rock samphire is a useful diuretic and helps to prevent flatulence, but as a disappointed Thratta has discovered, the plant is only really efficacious if harvested in late summer when one can extract the oils from the seeds. In the end, her otherwise useless plants ended up with the mule-train's cook, for samphire can be sprinkled with salt and boiled to make a good pickle.

If she wants to continue her career as a herbalist, Thratta must learn to distinguish at a glance between each of the 500 or so medicinal plants growing in the region, the uses of each and how to recognize the eighty or so that resemble those used for medicine but which are instead poisonous to some degree or another. Overall, around one in ten of the plants and bushes growing in the region has a purpose, either culinary, medicinal or both. Even with her current basic level of knowledge, Thratta knows that any country walk will never be the same again.

Moodily, she puts aside a sprig of Italian viper's bugloss (a key ingredient in poultices used to treat rheumatism). It seems she is destined to become a herbalist whether she likes it or not, and ponders whether she could not have picked a more relaxing profession as a disguise. Yet there is this much to be said for herbalists – they are often of exotic origins, so Thracians, Cappadocians or Phrygians are relatively common, and the secretive nature of their profession means that herbalists often go veiled or cloaked.

For example, it's not unusual for bashful customers to ask for *philtre* – love potions – for which Thratta's mistress supplies a mixture of cyclamen and mandrake served in wine. If the potion is successful, even more bashful young ladies might come in later seeking a draught made from *Daphne oleoides* with which to prevent pregnancy. Occasionally someone might hint at the need for monkshood ('to, um, poison a dog') and such persons are sent away with instructions never to return, for a herbalist in possession of this deadly plant may rightly be considered an accessory to murder if the plant is misused. Overall, handing over herbs has consequences and there are plenty of reasons why a herbalist might prefer not to be readily identified, which suits Thratta just fine.

That said, it was certainly more fun back when she was sorting and mixing herbs in the courtyard of her adoptive aunt in Halicarnassus. Old Eudoxia is determined to pass on her decades of learning and has no interest in merely providing shelter for a runaway slave – in fact, the normally gossipy old lady is extremely careful not to ask any questions at all about where Thratta has come from.

Instead, late into the night she imbibes beaker after beaker of cheap Icarian wine and tells Thratta long, rambling yarns about her girlhood and family in Phrygia. It was only after she had been forced to listen to several evenings of such stories that it finally dawned on Thratta that she was being given the sort of background detail for her role that she will require should she ever be questioned about her origins by the authorities. If needs be, the old herbalist can be wilfully ignorant, but she is certainly not stupid.

Tonight, Thratta's potions will be tested and found unsatisfactory and she will pay close attention to how and why each potion is a failure, because the old lady is patient with first-time mistakes and carefully explains exactly how to rectify them. A second identical error earns Thratta a sharp rebuke and a rap across the ankles with the knobbly old cane with which the woman gets around. After a bad evening, Thratta sometimes hobbles back to her tent wondering how Eudoxia's first apprentice was able to run away, when she can barely walk.

Tomorrow she will be up just before dawn to prowl the cliff-edge where the salt wind from the sea blows across the road. There will be Syrian rhubarb growing in rocky crevices sheltered from the wind [taken internally, good for ulcers, haemorrhoids and constipation] and wall germander [used as a decoction for kidney pain] on the slopes. Eventually she will have gathered enough material in her woven basket to sit and enjoy a hunk of bread and cheese while she waits for the mule train to catch up with her.

She will show her instructor what she has collected and will be informed that she has gathered the plants from unsuitable locations at the wrong time of day and that the plants were at the wrong stage of maturity anyway. Then Eudoxia will show her samples of what she should have gathered and from where, and if she has missed a particularly valuable herb Thratta will have to miss lunch as she scurries back to make up for the omission. The afternoon will be spent watching Eudoxia prepare materials, all the while learning herbs, their uses and how to compound them. Then in the evening Thratta does homework, putting together what she has learned.

The days are flying by and sometimes Thratta wonders why it is that when her mistress used to beat her in Athens she felt anger and resentment, but when Eudoxia raps her painfully across the shins she feels only mild chagrin and regret that she has let her teacher down yet again.

The Sprinter

Symilos the sprinter is not married, but even if he were, his relationship with his *gymnastes* (personal trainer) would be closer than with any spouse. In fact, as many an athlete's wife has discovered to her indignation, it is often the *gymnastes* who decides when and how often a wife can have sex with her husband.

It was not always so. Once upon a time, they say athletes bathed only in rivers and springs and were accustomed to sleeping on the ground or on straw pallets that they gathered for themselves from the fields. They dined on

GREEK GYMNASIUMS

Few things identified a city as Greek more clearly than its gymnasiums. This is unsurprising, because many other Mediterranean societies had cultural objections to public nudity, which is what gymnasiums were all about. While the modern gym is usually an indoor space filled with sweaty jocks, the Greek version was usually an open outdoor area discreetly screened by buildings (changing rooms, baths etc.) and trees. In Athenian gymnasiums, at least, time was set aside in the mornings for schoolchildren to use the facilities for exercise, wrestling and academic studies. The Greeks believed that the mind should be exercised along with the body, and gymnasiums were also frequented by philosophers and teachers of rhetoric. Socrates liked to spend his days hanging around in the gym disputing with all comers. One of his students, called Plato, made his favourite gymnasium such a place of learning that the name of that facility – the Academy – is now more associated with intellectual and cultural exertions than the physical kind.

barley bread or unleavened loaves made from unsifted wheat and after exercise they rubbed themselves down with oil from wild olives.

Then, some 400 years ago, along came the literal spoilsport Epicarmo of Sicily, who decided that the natural

WRESTLERS IN ACTION

ability of an athlete could be vastly improved by training and preparation. By way of proof there was Dromeus of Stymphalos, a distance runner who reportedly swept every competition in which he participated. The Pythian Games, the Isthmian and the Nemean: he won them all, time and again, by the unfair technique of actually practising for them. He also added plenty of meat to his diet whereas formerly athletes had made do with cheese fresh from the basket.

So nowadays no one can even think of participating in the Olympics without a strenuous training regime beforehand. Fortunately, most of the skills needed for athletic competition are close to what a warrior needs for warfare, so any settlement with pretensions to being a city has a gymnasium where the men can train. As the word gymnasium means 'naked exercise', women are generally excluded from the premises, though, as always, the Spartans like to be the exception and physical fitness is as prized among their young women as it is with the boys.

Since he has declined the offer of citizenship in Crete, it is probable that once he retires from competition Symilos will take up a post as resident trainer at a gymnasium such as this one in Lindos where he is temporarily resident.

While cities lavishly praise Olympic winners, civic memories are short and there are plenty of tales of former victors, now aged, who hobble about in ragged cloaks largely forgotten by their fellow citizens. The best way to avoid such a fate is to have a lucrative training contract arranged with a gymnasium before retirement looms, and there are numerous cities that would happily ensconce Symilos in the position of head trainer of their most prestigious establishment.

Symilos has read Plato – partly because his trainer believes that physical fitness and mental clarity go together – and has observed that even that great philosopher described several famous champions who became coaches. Plato had also taken on board the teaching of Epicarmo of Sicily and argued for a rigorous training regime as the foundation for sporting success.

With his second career in mind, Symilos not only pays attention to what his *gymnastes* is coaching him but also how he does it. A top personal trainer – and naturally, Symilos hires only the best – does not simply arrive with a set of exercises in mind but instead prepares a training regime after a careful study of his subject's physical and mental state. It is not unusual for an athlete to start training with several previous injuries on record and a good trainer takes account of this and tries to strengthen the damaged limbs rather than exacerbate the previous harm.

In short, a good trainer must have mastered some very specific elements of physiology, human biology, ergonomics and sports medicine. The rewards are substantial, for no one underestimates the role of a good *gymnastes* in an athlete's victory. When the great eulogist Pindar wrote his epic poems commemorating victors at the Games, he would frequently in the same breath mention the trainer and, indeed, many athletes when putting up commemorative inscriptions make sure that the role of their *gymnastes* is properly celebrated. It's not just the athletes who compete for glory.

So now Symilos reports to the *xystos*, a part of the gymnasium set aside for his training and notes rather gloomily that his trainer has arranged for a long strip of river sand to be laid down some two hand-spans deep. Today, evidently, will be focused on resistance training and breath control, with Symilos running at speed through the ankle-deep sand again and again until he is exhausted. It's a change from the total body workout he has been doing for the past four days, when his *gymnastes* has had him doing sit-ups, press-ups and light workouts with weights followed by long sessions of river swimming. If his trainer follows the regular schedule, in four days' time they'll move up to sprint training, when Symilos will practise for his event under conditions as close to the actual thing as possible.

The only consolation Symilos will allow himself as he

grunts and curses through the sand for the umpteenth time is that he will be allowed an extra flagon of wine after dinner tonight. The sand sprints make him sweat profusely and his *gymnastes*, like most other trainers, believes that the toxins from the wine are expelled from his body in his sweat.

While his trainer may appear to be intent on sadistically driving him to exhaustion, Symilos knows that the man will keep careful watch of his skin colour, his breathing and how coordinated he is in his running. As soon as his movements lose their smooth rhythm, the trainer will call a break, but woe betide Symilos if the *gymnastes* should believe he is faking – Symilos will still get his break but the exercises will double in intensity afterwards.

Two things keep Symilos hard at work through these brutal mornings. One is the bone-deep conviction that he has to do this to even have a chance at Olympic glory and the other is that – rather like hitting one's toe with a hammer – it is so nice when he stops.

The *apotherapia* – 'after-training' – would be a thoroughly pleasant experience even for a man who does not have a feeling of relief washing through his fast-relaxing body. For someone who does, and Symilos definitely will, the experience is almost heavenly. After a series of breathing exercises designed to take the strain from his heart, Symilos will lie on a cool, polished table and have the grime and sweat gently scraped off his body by his masseur, who does this with a small curved tool called a *strigil*. This is followed by a deep massage designed to relieve tight or knotted muscles, which leaves Symilos as limp as a rag doll, barely able to stagger to the customized bathing facilities beside the gym where he will enjoy a long, drowsy spell in the steam room.

After that, Symilos will take a dip in the cool water of a bath and finish with a brisk, refreshing swim in the nearby river. Then it's a late lunch, with a lot of fresh fruit and raw vegetables with nuts, and a large slab of lightly salted ham. Then Symilos will retire to his lounger and spend an hour or two taking in the healthy rays of the afternoon sun. Soon after sundown he will be in bed (alone), for his trainer believes that when an athlete is not working out he should be resting or sleeping, and if he has energy for anything else he is not training hard enough.

6

ΕΥΚΛΕΙΟΣ ΠΡΩΤΑ
ΒΗΜΑΤΑ
(March – First Steps)

The Bride

A contract, they say, should be a meeting of minds, in that the party of the first part has something that is desired by the party of the second part and that the party of the first part is willing to hand over according to the terms laid out in the contract. Or to put it another way, the maiden Apphia is desired by Kallipides of Elis and, if terms can be agreed, her father is willing to hand her over (in fact, in Apphia's jaundiced opinion, her father is not only willing to hand her over but disgustingly eager to do so).

Apparently, the question of whom Apphia would marry had resolved itself when Kallipides returned unexpectedly to the house while Apphia's sisters were visiting. Believing themselves alone, the four young women were dancing around the fountain in the courtyard, and not doing any old dance, but the *cordax* – a set of gyrations commonly performed by actors in the more vulgar sort of comedy. The actual dance involves lewd waggling of the buttocks, rotation of the hips and slapping one's thighs, in this case to the accompaniment of whoops of laughter by the participants.

Kallipides had entered unnoticed amid the general merriment and had remained quietly by the gate for almost a minute, standing as if thunderstruck. Then one of the sisters had seen him and the women had fled giggling to the shelter of their quarters. That evening, Kallipides had informed Apphia's father of his earnest desire to be wed and that details of a dowry could be dismissed as a mere technicality.

Well, not entirely dismissed because, as Kallipides had somewhat bashfully informed his hosts, he had a mother in Elis who was possessed of something of a strong personality and, should he not come home without at least a token sum, he was going to get a maternal earful on arrival. Besides, everyone knows that a good dowry is at least as much in the interest of Apphia as it is of benefit to Kallipides. For a start, it is not as if Apphia's eager suitor is desperately in need of money, for anyone who can afford to take a year's sabbatical in Athens to study philosophy is self-evidently not short of cash. Secondly, if the marriage should not work out and Apphia ends up divorced or widowed, that dowry will be returned to her as a shield between herself and a cruel world. Not that Apphia needs worry on that account, Kallipides assures her father, for

ATHENIAN METICS

Athens had a large population of foreigners who came to the city attracted by the commercial possibilities ('metic' is a short form of *meta-oikos:* 'one who changes homes') and some metics had lived in Athens for generations. Their long residence in the city had given them a recognized role in civic life, which is unsurprising as metics made up around a quarter of the non-slave population. Metics were almost invariably Greeks, though with a smattering of Phoenicians and Egyptians, and varied in social status from being ex-slaves (slaves were almost exclusively non-Athenian) to extremely wealthy merchants. Metics had to pay an extra tax for the privilege of living in Athens, and those involved in trade seem to have been liable for further duties. Metics could not own land, serve on juries or hold public office, but they had the same access to the courts as Athenian citizens and were liable for military service.

should anything happen to him – and may the gods avert such misfortune – then Apphia will be assured of a home with her new mother-in-law.

This prospective mother-in-law whom she has never met already arouses concern in Apphia, based only on the considerable trepidation with which her son speaks of her. Nevertheless, her doubts were partly assuaged by her sisters, who assure her that there are considerable advantages to having a husband who is accustomed to taking orders from his womenfolk. So it all comes down to this: how much is Apphia's father prepared to pay this stranger from Elis to take a surplus daughter off his hands?

Yet a dowry of at least moderate substance must be found, if not as a legal requirement then as a social obligation. There is also a general expectation that the size of a woman's dowry reflects her status in the household and her subsequent influence in family matters. As a general rule, a wife's dowry should be about 10 per cent of her husband's overall wealth but everyone knows that this target is unobtainable in Apphia's case.

On the other hand, by marriage to Apphia, the family of Kallipides cements the bond between the two families in Elis and Athens respectively. While Kallipides may

Wedding preparations

not care much for such matters, Apphia's father is aware that his guest's formidable mother might be interested in having an inside man in Athenian business affairs – for example, in finding a lucrative outlet for her farm's superb goat's milk cheeses.

Apphia's father is therefore keen that the marriage goes ahead, especially as Kallipides has announced his intention to remain in Athens to continue his studies until at least the end of summer, which means that his daughter will be living nearby and her family will be on hand to help her transition into married life.

Following their guest's declaration of intent, Apphia waited as her parents settled down to a detailed look at the household finances and reached an agreement. Namely that, her mother's family permitting, Apphia's dowry will be that which her mother brought into her marriage, a fine set of gold ornaments and precious stones that has rested untouched in a strongbox in the matrimonial bedroom for the past three decades. Then, over the coming years, this will be replaced, for Apphia's father is not getting any younger and that dowry will be needed should the mother be widowed.

To all this, Kallipides displayed a fine disdain – presumably not because he despises the dowry, but because in many ways it is of much greater benefit to Apphia than it is to himself. She knows it keeps her family invested in the well-being of their daughter and maintains their prestige in the metic community. Kallipides explained that personally, he would be happy enough just to be married to the girl who has impressed him so deeply, though when he said as much he was rather taken aback by his prospective mother-in-law's fierce reaction. Was it not Plato, she had demanded, who wanted women's dowries abolished because having the backup of a dowry made a wife less servile in a marriage? Was it a partner the Elean wanted or a mere concubine?

Naturally, Kallipides has no idea that the main sticking point in an otherwise mutually desirable match between the two families is his 'barbarous' accent. As a properly decorous guest, Apphia notes he has refrained from so much as holding a conversation with his intended bride (though she suspects her wiggling buttocks may have been much on his mind). As a result, Kallipides has no idea of Apphia's feelings toward him and this appears to cause him no little anxiety. The father of a bride has a social responsibility to ensure that his daughter is properly betrothed to a suitable husband who will treat her well and, should the girl be deeply unhappy with her match, this will reflect badly on the parents. In theory, a bride has absolutely no say in whom she marries but everyone knows that in matters matrimonial, theory and reality often diverge.

The Builder

Time. Until now, Meton has never thought of time as an enemy, for by and large construction in the Greek world is a very leisurely business. Meton knows of one constructor on the island of Delos to whom the local authorities gave over four years simply to lay a relatively short stretch of pavement. The famed Parthenon of Athens was built at speed with all the resources of the Athenian empire behind the construction, yet even that building took just over fifteen years to complete. Meton has a temple to build and barely another seven months to do it in.

He is already behind time because one can't simply throw up a temple even if that temple is more or less a reassembly rather than an original construction. One has to gather the workers and the material, and it is a task requiring superhuman energy and patience just to get the human and inanimate resources together at the same time and organize them once they have arrived.

Take the carters, for example. Meton had assumed that he would be able to hire local farmers to transport the huge blocks of stone from one temple site to another. He has always done this in the past and encountered no difficulty, but has never tried to do so at the start of winter when every ox for miles around is needed for ploughing. It was almost the winter solstice before he was able to start transporting his stone and even once he had the oxen it was a slow and painful business. Usually one transports stone overland in July and August when the roads, though potholed and boulder-strewn, are at least not treacherously boggy morasses or mud-slick slopes. It took teams of twenty to thirty oxen to move each block of stone for the foundations, with each pair of oxen needing to be hired from grasping peasant farmers along the route. Even now, the stone is still slowly coming in at the rate of one or two blocks a day.

That said, the foundation stones of the temple are now in place – the close-hewn stones lying in the carefully excavated base that Meton had prepared for them, the massive blocks carefully held together with lead-protected metal clamps. Earth-shaking Poseidon has already destroyed this temple once and Meton is determined that, should the god try again, the rebuilt structure will give Poseidon a run for his money.

Assembling the foundation could be done with unskilled labour but for the next steps Meton has had to send out for a host of skilled workmen. Even before the first stones are laid, scaffolders have to be brought in and consulted on how the stone blocks will be hoisted into place. Craftsmen from Elis have immediately to set about crafting new ceramic tiles for the temple roof, since all the tiles of the old temple were either broken or scavenged by opportunistic locals. Metalworkers will be needed for more reinforcing clamps to hold the stone blocks together and for bronze fittings to be placed in the stone where decorative friezes will later be set. (Thankfully, the friezes themselves will generally show generic hunting scenes or elaborately intertwined vines – the sort of thing most decent stonemasons have in stock. Meton has already ordered a set wholesale from Corinth.) Later, sculptors will be needed for Serapis-specific reliefs and some votive-style statues and after that painters will go over the entire edifice to bring the statues and reliefs to life, and to add the usual vivid colours that give a temple its identity. Finally, goldsmiths and silversmiths will work on the cult statue of the god to whom all this effort is dedicated.

Because temples are an essential part of Greek civic life, there's always a floating population of workmen who spend their careers building them. These men go from one building site to another, moving freely between Greece, Egypt and the Hellenistic East, and all that Meton has to do is put the word out as to what kind of workers he needs and how many, and in dribs and drabs they will make their way to him from the Elean port of Pheia.

Fortunately, because he is salvaging a pre-built temple (one previous careless owner), Meton has been able to skip several of the usual preliminary steps. He has no need to hire an architect because he is also one himself and his temple obviously comes pre-designed anyway. Basically, he needs three classes of workers: carters and hauliers, craftsmen, and artists, and Meton is well aware that one of his major jobs will be arbitrating and settling conflicts between the three groups. The sculptor will demand a block of stone rough-hewn just so and the craftsman who installs it will angrily inform him that the imperfections in the stone make it impossible to meet these requirements because those bone-idle carters delivered the wrong block of stone and did it late so the sculptor will just have to make the best of it. And so on, and on and on.

As the architect, Meton has more to do than simply plan out the building. An *arkitekton* in Greece is more of a technician doubling as a site foreman. While he may not carve stonework or set it in place, it is Meton's job to make sure that those who do the work have done it exactly according to the very precise specifications given to each skilled worker in his contract. Just as Meton is liable to the Egyptian authorities if his work is shoddy or delayed, the workers whom Meton hires are liable if they produce substandard work or if they damage someone else's work in the process of doing their own. Bitter experience has also made Meton have each craftsman guarantee that should he leave unfinished any work he has been contracted to do, that craftsman is obligated to find someone to complete the task.

In one way, skilled contractors are not a major issue, for they are given only subsistence wages while on the job and are paid in full only when their part in the project has been successfully completed. More of a drain on Meton's finances are the *misthomata* – wages to unskilled labourers whom Meton pays at sundown each day. Just the number of carters needed to haul the stone into place is depleting his funds rapidly – a worrying omen for what may be to come.

Still, the foundation is in place and Meton has now completed the first crucial step, which is very literally a step. This is the lowest step of those leading up to the temple proper and getting this exactly right is very important. This is because the almost invisible outward curve on the steps sets the size of the mathematical ratios that affect every horizontal surface on the building. Such curvature is necessary because the human eye perceives a long, straight line as sagging inward, so the building has to be subtly bowed in the opposite direction to appear straight.)

Building any temple is a race between the construction of the temple and the depletion of the funds available for the job. Here, beside the Olympic *stadion*, Meton feels it's only right that his particular race should also be a sprint.

The Merchant

Once a merchant, always a merchant, and while passing through Antioch from Sidon, Sakion found an opportunity to make his trip to Pergamon still more profitable. While he was in Antioch, a caravan had arrived from the east and among the goods were little earthen jars packed with peppercorns from India and vases of opium from Mesopotamia. Sakion promptly purchased both peppercorns and opium as a job lot, for he knows of a dealer in Brundisium who can shift the opium to markets across Italy, and one can sell pepper anywhere – the stuff is like gold, only tastier and much lighter. The only problem is that these new purchases, together with the cargo of silk Sakion was already transporting, means that the merchant now has assembled a collection of portable and highly expensive goods that would make any enterprising gang of brigands rich for life.

The land route from Antioch to Pergamon involves travel through the Anti-Taurus Mountains and the wild lands of Cilicia and Caria. From there, things would normally get a bit better as one follows the old Persian royal road from Laodicia to Sardis and then past Thyatira to Pergamon. Unfortunately, that's no longer the case because the Celtic Galatians who have established themselves in the Anatolian highlands around Ankyra have become a major nuisance – so major, in fact, that Eumenes, the ruler of Pergamon, pays the Galatians not to attack his towns and farms. Sadly no one has ever managed to persuade the Galatians that trade caravans are not fair game and even if the Galatian tribal leaders were so persuaded, the message would not percolate down to the wild young men who do most of the raiding.

It's now spring, with the worst of the winter storms only a bad memory, and the first merchant ships are tentatively setting sail across the safer stretches of Mediterranean coastal waters. It might even be safe to travel by sea but for one problem: brigands are not limited to the land and the coast between Antioch and Pergamon is infested with brigands of the sea – that is, by pirates.

Ever since the conquests of Alexander toppled kingdoms and upturned the lives of hundreds of thousands of people in Asia Minor and the Levant, piracy has been a problem. Fishermen and sometimes peasants who had never previously contemplated a life on the ocean wave were forced into piracy by desperate circumstances – and most found the profession far more rewarding than anyone had expected.

It does not help that far from trying to suppress piracy, some of the Hellenistic kings positively encourage it. Ptolemy II (of course) heads the cast of villains here, for in his struggles with the Seleucid kings he happily recruited pirates as freebooting mercenaries and turned them loose on the coast of Asia Minor on the basis that almost everyone thereabouts was no friend of Egypt anyway. Antigonus of Macedon is also far from innocent and made good use of pirate allies in his recent attempt to suppress an Athenian bid for independence (known as the Chremonidean War).

Probably the only people interested in suppressing piracy are the Rhodians because the island city-state of

PIRACY IN THE MEDITERRANEAN

Piracy had a long tradition in the ancient Mediterranean, and indeed many cities such as Athens and Argos were situated slightly inland precisely because of the threat of seaborne invaders. Apart from being something of a traditional occupation in such places as the coast of Cilicia, some piracy was state-sponsored, Polykrates of Samos being an early example, and Queen Teuta of Illyria a contemporary one. Ancient ships tended to hug the coastline and often beached overnight, and this made merchant ships especially vulnerable as the rocky coastlines of Greece and Anatolia had numerous inlets and bays where opportunistic raiders could lurk. Also, the rapidly growing economies of the Hellenistic states led to an explosion of trade and a consequent increase of predators upon that trade.

Rhodes is a trading nation and, as such, dependent on keeping the sea lanes open. The coastal cities of Cnidos and Cos also join in anti-piracy operations, as does the island of Delos, though the latter may fairly be accused of hypocrisy as it does a booming trade in slaves, many of whom are unransomed pirate captives.

From the point of view of Sakion the merchant, his choices appear to be between taking a high risk of being robbed on land or taking a similar risk of being robbed at sea, with the latter option including a bonus opportunity

Merchant ship of the classical era

for death by drowning. Nevertheless, Sakion has opted to charter a ship from Antioch for two reasons. Firstly, it is much faster, and secondly, because he has been unwell lately. The malaise he developed in Alexandria has not gone away.

Just before he left Egypt, Sakion was smitten with a severe fever accompanied by muscle pain and nausea. He struggled to recovery but was still as weak as a kitten when he set out for Sidon. Now a month after he was sure he was well on the road to recovery, the symptoms are intensifying again. Overall, if he must be prostrate with illness, Sakion would prefer that he be so on a bed in a ship's cabin than carried on a bumpy litter in a mule train.

For the first week, it seemed as though he had made the right choice, and as the rocky coastline of Caria passed smoothly by, Sakion blessed the gods for the smooth seas, gentle winds and a sky the pale blue of a robin's egg. Even his fever seemed to be abating with the clean sea air. Though mooring close to shore at night, the captain kept their ship well out to sea during the day, standing well off from the nameless villages that lie in the uncountable coves and inlets of the coast of Caria. Today, on one such clear morning, Sakion was startled to hear the ship's captain unexpectedly utter a string of oaths and order the crewmen to pile on sail, something the men did with alacrity.

A panicked look around revealed no imminent danger. A few fishing boats lay between the merchantman and the coast but none of them appeared to be threatening, or large enough to present a threat even if they tried. In fact, two boats had hauled in their nets and were heading away from the merchantman at speed. Those boats were the problem, the captain explained once he had his vessel heading west as fast as its sails would permit. Having sighted a juicy merchantman, the fishing boats were headed for shore to round up allies.

It was almost midday before Sakion saw what the captain meant. A set of three dots on the horizon turned with disconcerting speed into small, fast, open-decked galleys of the type known as *aphractes* – vessels useless for fishing or carrying cargo, but ideal for rapidly transporting fifty or so men toward a floating target.

A stern chase is among the most nerve-wracking of naval encounters, not least because there is nothing to take the quarry's mind off the doom inexorably approaching from behind. Once all sail has been set and the ship is running before the wind, there's little else to do but settle down at the stern-rail and watch the sleek oar-powered galleys closing in. It is an odd experience – Sakion can eat a meal, talk with his servants and generally act as he does every day, but with the knowledge that in about an hour everything will descend into chaos and his life will be changed forever – if, that is, the pirates are in the mood to take prisoners. If they're not, Sakion's life will end then and there.

The pirate galleys inch closer and a despairing Sakion orders his servants to prepare to hoist his cargo overboard, on the basis that, if he is to lose everything, the loss is better sacrificed to Poseidon than seized by pirates. This course of action is firmly vetoed by the captain because firstly, if the pirates find that their long chase has been for naught, they will take out their frustration on passengers and crew in imaginative and acutely painful ways. Secondly, there is still a chance of escape. This is because the captain's precaution of standing well off from the coast has caused the pirates to row longer and harder than normal and they, the prey, have been blessed with a following wind. The merchantman can sail for as long as the breeze blows – but eventually the pirates giving chase will run out of puff.

A shout from the bow obliterates this last hope, for a crewman has noticed an approaching group of some dozen galleys that, on sighting the merchantman, have dropped sails and are heading straight for them under oars with evidently predatory intent. So now to keep fleeing from the pirates behind means sailing at full speed into the arms of the enemy ahead.

The despairing captain is about to order his crew to lower the merchantman's sails and to prepare to surrender when his keen eyes note something that completely changes the situation. The bow waves of the approaching ships have that distinct hump that signifies an underwater ram. This means that the approaching galleys, every bit as fast and sleek as the pirate ships behind, are friendlies – more specifically, they are *phylakides* – Rhodian ships designed specifically to counter the pirate menace.

Now the pirates have spotted the avenging *phylakides* too and there's considerable disorder as the panicked former predators try desperately to swing away from the sudden threat and run for the shore. But the Rhodian patrol vessels are fresh and the pirates already tired from their long pursuit of the merchantman. It will be a one-sided race and, buoyed by his sudden change in fortune, Sakion settles down at the ship's rail to watch. This is one stern chase that he intends to really enjoy.

The Lyre Player

An invitation to a symposium is something to be handled as carefully as if the messenger has deposited a sleeping wildcat into the recipient's arms. Perhaps the beast is, after all, a well-tamed pussycat who wants nothing more than to be petted and purr – or perhaps it will turn out to be a spitting fiend whose teeth and claws will mark the victim for life.

When considering attending a symposium, the first but not necessarily the most important question for an invitee

A FLUTE PLAYER ENTERTAINS SYMPOSIUM GUESTS

is who is hosting the occasion, and why? Certainly it is a compliment to be invited to such an affair, for it suggests that you are an intimate friend of the host. For the same reason, should you decline the invitation, this implies that you are also spurning your host's offer of friendship and doing so in a rather insulting manner. Who goes to whose symposia is a staple of city gossip and, given the constant rivalries and backbiting of any city's elites, attending one person's event is certain to offend that person's rivals and enemies – some of whom may be even more influential and powerful than the host.

Secondly, there's the matter of what sort of symposium it will be. Some are earnest affairs that serve basic foodstuffs and wine-tinged water while the attendees plunge deep into the intricacies of moral philosophy. At the other extreme, a symposium might be when one of the young aristocrats of the city decides to throw a no-holds-barred party with two prostitutes to a guest, unwatered wine by the bucketful, furniture thrown out of the windows and the city watch called to break up brawls on the premises. Reputations are easily lost at either type of gathering, whether one is seen to flounder while trying to get to grips with the stoic pronouncements of Chrysippus or seen floundering in the firm grip of law enforcement while en route to the cells.

Fortunately, there's another kind of symposium, where like-minded men gather amicably to sort out matters of importance to themselves and the city, whether the meeting be to decide who will stand in the next elections or the exact wording of a city council decree. Or perhaps the symposium might be called in consequence of a message from the island of Rhodes that a merchantman will soon be docking in Pergamon with a valuable cargo of silk, opium and pepper, and the city's businessmen want to arrange an amicable distribution of the goods without any of that tiresome bidding for the spoils that can so reduce profits.

By mutual agreement, the host (properly called the symposiarch) will be one Epigenes, for not only is he one of the city's leading traders but also his son is doing well in politics and has the ear of the royal heir presumptive, young Attalus. Furthermore, Epigenes has an excellent wine cellar, a superb chef and one of the best lyre players in western Anatolia to serenade the gathering. It will be an exclusive affair – just some fourteen invitees, though naturally the dining room in the *andron* of Epigenes (the *andron* is the part of the house reserved for male activities) has couches to accommodate twice that number.

The lyre player is of course Kallia and, rather unusually for a Hellenistic symposium, she will be the only woman present for the event. Aristocratic ladies generally retire to the women's quarters on these occasions and their place on the dining couches is taken instead by *hetairai*. *Hetairai* occupy a distinct place in aristocratic society, often able to keep up with the menfolk in conversation, political nous and wine consumption but also expected to supply sexual services once the party has passed a certain stage.

There's a limited supply of *hetairai* in even such an extensive city as Pergamon, however, and on this occasion the merchants don't particularly want their stitching up of the market to become common knowledge at other dinner parties, so the chatty *hetairai* have been dispensed with in favour of some highbrow music.

Kallia is not present for the first part of the meeting when the guests arrive, some freshly bathed, others glowing with oil after an afternoon's exertions at the gymnasium. She is sitting in her room carefully tuning the *barbitos* she will be playing on this occasion. A business affair this may be but it's still a symposium and she can expect wine to be splashed about, and – since she will be sitting near the door – the occasional half-drunken individual bumping into her on the way to the latrines. So Kallia is not going to expose her precious *kithara* to this uncouth environment and has instead opted to use a *barbitos* – a somewhat cruder instrument more suitable for the occasion.

The *barbitos* has a more 'erotic' voice, in that it is usually tuned an octave lower than the *kithara* and the longer, thicker strings can draw deep, mellow notes from the considerably larger soundbox. Kallia has taken this into account and will play in a key suited to the deeper voices of the men who will be able to join in the familiar hymn that marks the end of eating for the evening and the start of the drinking.

Kallia leaves her room and makes her way to the *andron*, waiting by the doorway as two slaves depart, carrying between them the table on which the evening's repast was served. The couches within are arranged against three walls facing the door and the dining table had formerly occupied the central space into which Kallia now walks, strumming the *barbitos*.

As she picks her way through the melodic theme, the symposiarch holds out a large drinking vessel – a *kylix* – to a slave boy who hastens to fill it from the large krater (wine vase) that has accompanied Kallia into the room, borne by the same two slaves who have just exited with the table.

The traders gathered in the room are musically literate enough to pick up on the riff Kallia plays on the well-known hymn to Hermes, the god of merchants, but she sings the song through so that everyone is clear on the lyric and melody:

Oh, you of the winged sandals, friend of humanity, who understands the words of mortal men

Who speaks for the gods and rejoices in skilful athletics and smooth deceit

*Fluent interpreter, master of trade, you soothe our troubles
    away*

*Your herald's staff a symbol of blameless peace, O god of
    profits,*

Happy one, the luck-bringer, the teller of tales

Hear our prayers, bring our lives to a peaceful end

*Well-stocked with long memories of a good livelihood and
    well-spoken words.*

(ORPHIC HYMN TO HERMES L7-12)

Then Kallia pauses, picks her way once again through the
introductory notes and accompanies the symposiarch as
he sings the first line. As he does so, the symposiarch spills
some wine to the floor as a libation to Hermes, then passes
the cup to the next participant who accompanies Kallia in
the second line and makes his own libation. So it continues
until the *kylix* has been passed around the entire group
and each has sung his part. Kallia moves from guest to
guest, smiling encouragement as she sings, and takes care
to step carefully over the rivulets of wine that trickle to a
drain in the centre of the room (*andron* floors are designed
to cope with large amounts of liquid).

The symposium proper – the drinking part – has
now begun, though the financial discussions continue in
earnest as Kallia sits herself on a backless chair and eases
the protagonists into the second part of their evening with
a well-known theatrical number. Later, as the business part
of the party winds down, she tries some popular marching
songs while the guests take turns at endeavouring to

extemporize on the chorus.

After this, she provides dramatic sound effects as the guests play at *kottabos*, a game where the last drinker from the communal *kylix* swirls the sediment of the wine dregs about in the cup and hurls it at a target in the centre of the room. Kallia gives a dramatic build-up as the drinker winds up his throw and plays either an off-key flat for a miss or a triumphal paean if the dregs hit their target, and the thrower is rewarded with applause and a prize of sweetmeats or cakes.

As midnight passes, she drops into a sleepy, contemplative mode, extemporizing tunes and exploring gentle musical themes as one by one the guests rise from their couches and gently stagger to the door, summoning their attendants from the courtyard as they take their leave of the symposiarch. Overall, reflects Kallia, as she plays the last guest out of the *andron*, there are worse ways to spend an evening.

7

ΑΡΤΕΜΙΣΙΟΣ ΔΥΣΚΟΛΙΕΣ

(April – Setbacks)

ഇഇഇഇഇഇഇഇഇഇഇഇഇഇഇഇഇഇഇഇഇഇഇഇ

The Farmer

Winter wheat is a perilous crop, for humans are but the last in a long line of creatures that want to eat it. The problems start as soon as the seed is sown, for birds follow the sower, and grain that is meant to find a home in the autumnal soil often instead finds a home in a partridge, grouse or other avian crop predator. Even when the seed grain is in the ground it is certainly not safe. Fungi, worms and rot can ruin a crop unseen, even as the farmer surveys his fields unaware that nothing but weeds are going to sprout. Then, should the first tender shoots appear, starving deer emerge from the woods in February ready to devastate the crop once again. As the crop grows and strengthens, grubs chew up the roots, and bruchid beetles drop their larvae into the developing ears of grain. It is every farmer's nightmare that just as a crop is ready for harvest the wind will bring a cloud of locusts that settle on the field in their countless numbers and reduce a season's work to naught in the space of an afternoon.

Let us say, however, that a farmer has avoided these disasters through good luck or careful preparation (and usually the farmer needs both of these things). Then there is only the problem of a slow, wet spring turning too soon into a halcyon fortnight of warm, sunny weather before the drizzle closes in again. This is certain to hit the developing crop with white, powdery patches of mildew, and the earlier the mildew hits, the higher it moves up the plant and the more the crop will be damaged.

Yet mildew results only in fewer and smaller kernels of wheat. What every farmer dreads is finding that the crop is infested with tiny drumstick-shaped spores of ergot, and again the wetter the spring the more likely the chances of an ergot outbreak. Ergot occurs more frequently with open-flowering crops, such as rye, but it is just as devastating when it takes hold in winter wheat.

Ergot does not prevent a full crop from being harvested, but only in the most desperate of times would any sane human consider eating such a crop – partly because he will not remain sane for long afterwards. Eating ergot-contaminated food causes wild hallucinations, skull-splitting headaches and delirium often followed by gangrene and death. Unsurprisingly, the local authorities get somewhat bitter with a farmer who allows a contaminated crop to reach market, and as ergot spores

DEMETER, GODDESS OF THE CORN AND
HER DAUGHTER PERSEPHONE, RIGHT, GODDESS
OF SEASONAL RENEWAL

survive in the soil for up to a year, it is not unusual for that field to compulsorily lay fallow for the next two years or so – even if anyone can be persuaded to eat that farmer's crops ever again.

Iphita is well aware of all these dangers and, like every farmer, she does what she can to mitigate possible damage, taking care to spread the risk. Parasites tend to be specific in their choice of victim so a blight that hits the wheat crop is unlikely to damage her pulses, and vice versa. Also, nothing beats regular inspection of the fields and the ruthless purging of any plants showing the first signs of damage or infection.

Even so, Iphita's precautions began well before the first seed grains hit the soil. Firstly, the wood ash from the previous year's domestic fires had been carefully collected and later spread on the fields, for wood ash is both a natural fertilizer and great for discouraging insects. When the first winter rain falls, the ash turns to lye and dilutes through the soil, killing larval spores and weed roots. Then before the soil is seeded, Iphita ploughs in the abundant manure that her oxen and farmworkers have been producing through the summer and adds to this carefully ground eggshell, which she has been collecting for this purpose all year long, for eggshell somehow moderates the effect of the wood ash.

Then, before being scattered on the soil, the seeds have been carefully bathed in a mixture of leek juice (pulverized leek in water or urine as preferred) and amurca, the bitter watery sediment that filters out of olive oil that has been left to stand for a long time. As well as being a useful weedkiller, amurca is a handy food preservative and firewood dipped in the stuff is considerably less smoky. Many swear that doses of amurca cure everything from gout to rheumatism, and though dubious of such claims, Iphita has to admit it works well with skin infections and preserving seed from bugs.

When the winter emmer wheat crop was finally sown, the proper sacrifices were made to Demeter and the small gods of the harvest, and everyone had taken the day off on the sixth day of the month, which is notoriously bad for anything to do with plants. While keeping Demeter and other supernatural entities onside is self-evidently necessary, Iphita gave the corn goddess some help by scattering other seeds into her crop as soon as the last winter frosts allowed. So amid the wheat, oregano and dill are sprouting along with marjoram and garlic. All pungent oily plants seem to have a smell that discourages weevils and other insect pests, and a few herbs along with the harvest never go amiss.

Even so, it is proverbial that 'some days are mothers, but others are stepmothers', and it was on a stepmotherly day that a mighty thunderstorm came sweeping in from the sea along with powerful, capricious winds that blew the wheat this way and that. This time it was not Iphita's precautions that saved the crop, but those of her husband's grandfather – he who had planted the stands of sturdy oak that broke the force of the winds as they swirled about Mount Kronos and rushed down on the crop in stalk-flattening gusts.

No farmer will ever admit to having a good crop until the harvest is in, yet as she prowls the field edges, looking for broken fences or tunnels dug by hungry rodents, Iphita cautiously has to admit that things are looking good. Of course, even once the emmer wheat has been harvested and winnowed, the problems will not end there. Iphita has commissioned a potter to make huge amphorae to store her grain – pots that make up in craftsmanship what they lack in aesthetics.

Once the grain has been poured into these pots, the lids will be sealed with wet clay to make them airtight. Without wind or other air currents to disperse it, the grain slowly exhales that gas that Demeter has breathed into it, and the breath of the goddess of grain is inimical to living things, including weevils and other bugs, which might have been planning on breeding in otherwise ideal conditions.

Having satisfied herself that her gamble on winter wheat appears to be paying off, Iphita takes herself down to the fields beside the river to ruefully regard the disaster zone that is her chickpeas. The same damp spring that is fattening the ears of her emmer wheat has been less kind to this winter crop. Early inspection caught the purple bruises on the chickpea flowers that signal an *asochyta* fungal blight, and Iphita had immediately purged the infected corner of the field.

Unfortunately, the same windstorm that came close to flattening the wheat crop seems to have propagated the *asochyta* spores across the field. From where she stands, Iphita can see weak and wilting leaf stems and formerly green, healthy leaves turning pale yellow. Inevitably the chickpeas will collapse, taking the fungal spores into the ground as they go. Iphita shrugs and offers a brief prayer of thanks that at least her lentils have survived. After the fungal blight, the field will be useless for chickpeas for at least three years, but that should not affect the spring vegetables that Iphita plans on sowing as soon as the useless chickpeas have been ploughed back into the soil.

The Diplomat

Messages can be intercepted and read, but it's much harder to read the messenger. As a result, the written missive that the diplomat Persaeus is preparing for his king is more of an aide-memoire for the messenger who will deliver a longer and much more comprehensive verbal report. Since there is little doubt that the text part of his report will be intercepted and read by Seleucid spies, the dispatch that Persaeus is currently composing is as much for the benefit of the Seleucid royal court as it is for the diplomat's royal master back in Macedon.

Persaeus chews moodily on the end of his reed pen as he scans what he has written so far. Firstly, he has reported that the Seleucid king is in good health and seems ready to endure the rigours of another campaigning season. Although King Antiochus II the God has not yet chosen to reveal to his followers against whom this campaign will be directed. Macedon need not fear any hostile activity, however, for the Seleucid empire and Macedon are both determined to maintain their warm friendship.

All well and good, though the messenger who takes the report to Macedon will also add that it is Persaeus' opinion that King Antiochus is drinking far more than is good for him. It is not just damage to the royal liver that concerns Persaeus; it is more the fact that heavy drinking has other ramifications. The Seleucid royal court are all of Macedonian stock and, as such, are accustomed to punishing the wine flasks in their leisure time, but they are also hard, brutal men who have little tolerance for weakness in anyone, including their monarch.

A king who is seen as too flawed to execute his royal duties properly is very likely to suffer an unexpected fatal fall from his horse, a sudden heart attack in the bath or a straightforward sword thrust through the intestines. For a Hellenistic monarch, any of the above count as death by natural causes – it's dying of old age in bed that's unnatural. In short, then, the king's drinking habit is extremely unhealthy for reasons that have little to do with his health.

Another reason why Antiochus is unlikely to reach a mellow old age is because the king is planning to leave his current unhappy marriage and return to his first wife, Laodice. Not only is this certain to infuriate the Egyptians, but it is also going to spell the ruin of those members of the royal court who have been backing Berenice, the current queen. If Berenice gives birth to a boy (and considering the state of the relationship between the king and his royal wife, it's a wonder that conception occurred at all) then those powerbrokers who back Berenice will scent an opportunity. It's not hard to imagine a scenario where Berenice gives birth to a boy, and then before the king can divorce her, he suffers a fatal accident. This would leave

Berenice as regent for her infant son and those power-hungry men who back her the de facto rulers of the empire. That such a situation might arise is more than possible, for Persaeus has already received delicate enquiries as to how Macedon might react should such an event come to pass.

On the subject of delicate enquiries, there's also the matter of Laodice, the king's former wife and possible wife-to-be. Persaeus knows she is well aware that the Hellenistic game of thrones is every bit as deadly for the womenfolk as it is for the men. Should Antiochus die abruptly while still married to Berenice, then Laodice and her children will die also – so promptly that their first intimation that Antiochus is dead will be when the executioners come for her and her offspring.

So, Laodice is keen that her ex-husband repudiate Berenice as soon as possible and return to the loving arms of his ex-wife. If this does come to pass, Laodice will understandably be keen to lock in her gains. After all, Antiochus has repudiated her once for political reasons and there is nothing to prevent him doing so again – unless, that is, he suffers a sudden and fatal attack of indigestion shortly after the happy reconciliation.

Should that happen, it will be Laodice who becomes regent for her young son and it will be Berenice and her newborn child who meet the executioners. All Laodice needs before she sets things in motion are assurances of Macedon's support once Antiochus the God departs this mortal plane, probably soon after enjoying an intimate dinner with his wife, who has very discreetly informed the diplomat of all this.

WHAT BECAME OF ANTIOCHUS THE GOD?

As Persaeus had feared, Antiochus' queen, Berenice, gave birth to a healthy son, thus making Ptolemy II grandfather to the heir apparent of the Seleucid empire. It seems that Antiochus was also uneasy about this development and, in 246 BC, two years after our imagined visit by Persaeus, Antiochus renounced Berenice and returned to live with his former wife. That former wife had by now laid her plans carefully and, in a simultaneous coup, Antiochus was killed by poison while Berenice and her infant son were killed in Antioch. The young Seleucus II (Antiochus' eldest son) was declared king, with the grieving widow acting as regent while the outraged Ptolemies set about preparing a war of revenge. All of which, from the point of view of the Macedonians, was highly satisfactory.

One way or another, the outlook for Antiochus II of the Seleucids is grim, and Persaeus needs to warn his royal master in Macedon that the Seleucid empire is likely to suffer an abrupt change in management within the next year or two. Picking up his pen once more, Persaeus dips it into his well of ink (a mixture of soot and glue diluted with water) and inscribes more of his report on the papyrus, certain that King Antigonus will read between the lines what his diplomat is actually saying:

We believe the birth of a royal heir is imminent and that the gods will look kindly upon the event. [If our prayers are answered, Berenice will perish in childbirth, taking her newborn brat to Hades with her.]

Despite his delight at becoming a father yet again, His Divine Majesty remains considerate and mindful of his former wife, and makes every effort to reassure her that she is not excluded from his affections. [Antiochus wants to get back with Laodice as soon as he can work out how to ditch Berenice without starting a war with Egypt.]

As ever, it is without doubt your intention to offer fraternal support to a fellow monarch and I am sure Your Royal Majesty is already considering Macedon's joyful response now that Antiochus' much-loved wife has given birth. [Is there any way we can speed up the king's divorce before the pro-Berenice faction assassinates him?]

I am sure that Berenice's royal father in Egypt is also delighted with this news, and the fact that the succession in the Seleucid empire will pass to his grandson. [You do know the stakes here, don't you, sir?]

These close family ties can only bring the three Hellenistic kingdoms closer together in fraternal and paternal love, and bring about peace in our time. [If we don't do something about Berenice soon, Laodice is going to be killed and Antiochus won't go back to her. Then Egypt and the Seleucids won't go to war and Ptolemy will have

his daughter as regent in the Seleucid empire while
he continues to make life unbearable for us in Greece.
Things are not looking good.]

Persaeus finishes his report with the usual flowery
effusions, and hands it to a messenger who has already
been fully briefed on the subtext. Then, with a sigh, the
diplomat picks up his pen once more and prepares to write
an even more delicate message with an even more obscure
subtext. Basically, he needs full plausible deniability while
he informs Laodice that Macedon will push Antiochus to
reconcile with her – and once that happens, she should
make sure that her potions are ready.

〰〰〰〰〰〰〰〰〰〰〰〰〰〰〰〰〰〰〰〰〰

The Runaway

Despite the fact that the resin looks like something
dropped by an incontinent rabbit, myrrh is an excellent
material with many uses. It's also difficult for an itinerant
herbalist to gather, not least because the *commiphora* bushes
from which myrrh is harvested are jealously guarded by
those whose land they grow on. That land is mostly on the
Red Sea side of Egypt, though attempts have been made
(with mixed success) to grow the bushes in Anatolia.

What's more, myrrh can't just be plucked from the
leaves, but rather, once a suitable plant has been located,
the harvester must push through the spiny branches to

the main stem of the bush, taking care to pierce the bark and go deep into the sapwood, but not so deep that the heartwood is reached. Once this has happened, the injured plant will slowly bleed a waxy resin, which coagulates over the wound.

After a few days, the resin hardens and can be scraped away and dried, after which it is ready for export. Most myrrh moves from the site of production up through the desert kingdom of Nabataea [in modern Jordan and northern Arabia] and from there to the Hellenistic world, especially to the Anatolian city of Smyrna, which has been both a producer and exporter of myrrh for so long that the city derives its name from the substance ('*smyrna*' is Greek for 'myrrh').

For the herbalist, myrrh is wonderful stuff, so long as one can find it or afford it once it has been located. The problem is compounded by the fact that others are after myrrh as well – for example, the Hebrews of Judea use it by the bucketload in ritual purifications and other religious ceremonies. Myrrh is also mixed with aloes and used in burials, for there is something in the substance that inhibits decay.

From a herbalist's point of view, this is one of the major reasons for using myrrh, for a septic infection can be regarded as decay happening at speed in living flesh, and a tincture of myrrh can slow or prevent such infection like nothing else. In dead flesh, such as pork or beef, myrrh is a handy food preservative, so herbalists have to fight with priests, mourning relatives and chefs to get their hands on it.

The Cryptoportus of the ancient agora at Smyrna

Burned in the air – often together with (equally expensive) frankincense – myrrh seems able to inhibit the spread of disease in crowds. Myrrh is also very effective in dealing with oral infections so long as those swilling the stuff around their gums remember not to swallow, for myrrh is poisonous if taken internally at high concentration. Myrrh is also favoured by high-class courtesans, as genitals lightly oiled with myrrh not only smell pleasant, but also resist many of the parasites and other infections passed on by clients with substandard sexual hygiene.

In short, myrrh is extremely useful and correspondingly valuable, and since it is nowhere cheaper than in the wholesale markets of Smyrna, Eudoxia is keen to build up a stash of the material while the caravan is in that city, for not only will she use the myrrh in her own potions, but she also retails it to other herbalists whom she meets on her travels. Naturally, Eudoxia is far from being the only travelling herbalist who does this and consequently Smyrna has specialist merchants to cater for her needs.

It is because she had settled down in her tent for a prolonged bargaining session with one such dealer that Eudoxia had decided to send Thratta out into the market to search the stalls for other less precious materials nevertheless necessary for her craft. Even in springtime, by late afternoon the agora was crowded and sweaty, and Thratta was beginning to suffer under the heavy shawl she had wrapped around her neck and head. She was certainly not alone in her choice of headgear, for both Greek and Asiatic women tend to keep their heads covered when outside the house. Some other women do walk bareheaded and one blonde-headed lady, Thratta was delighted to see, carried an elaborate Thracian tattoo of an eagle on her neck.

Perhaps it was because no one in the crowd was paying her the slightest attention, or because she was tired and sweaty after being on her feet all day that Thratta finally decided to lose her shawl. The agora of Smyrna is located between the seaport and the theatre some 300 paces further uphill. This allows a pleasant breeze to blow in off the sea and up over the city's red-tiled roofs into the market, and gave Thratta a strong urge to let some of that deliciously cool air flow down her neck and over her chest. Or perhaps the loosening of her shawl had something to do with the fact that, as she was returning to Eudoxia's tent, she saw one of the caravan's muleteers, a rather comely young man in his late teens, and it had occurred to the girl that, by exposing some skin, she might prolong any conversation.

Indeed, the encounter with the young muleteer is going rather well, right up to the moment when rough hands suddenly grab Thratta by the shoulders and yank her away. The young man's indignant cries are ignored as Thratta is jostled toward a board upon which several notices are affixed. While outwardly yelling in distress, Thratta mentally curses herself for her complacency. It has been so long since anyone had even questioned her identity that she has started taking her anonymity for granted, even to the extent of ignoring the noticeboard and whatever messages it holds – and that despite the board being barely a stone's throw from Eudoxia's tent.

It is horribly clear what has happened. These men had read the descriptions of escaped slaves on the board and then barely had they stepped away than they encountered a young woman who exactly matches one of those descriptions. No wonder the men are dragging her back to the notice so that they can more precisely compare Thratta's description with their actual captive.

The men are not getting things all their own way. The young muleteer's shouts have drawn a crowd and there is considerable abuse being shouted at the two men holding Thratta. (Later, Thratta was to learn that this was because her captors were Hebrews and, at this time, Jews and Greeks get along like cats and dogs, and the crowd in the marketplace is largely Greek.)

An animated and largely incoherent shouting match follows in front of the noticeboard, with the Hebrews loudly insisting that they have captured an escaped slave, and Thratta and the young muleteer just as loudly insisting that they have not. Matters start to escalate towards a riot when the Hebrews attempt to pull off Thratta's chiton in order to discover whether her back is whip-scarred as the description maintains. Thratta resists with considerable vehemence, assisted by a growing band of supporters determined to preserve her modesty. These include some of the senior muleteers from Thratta's caravan who have arrived on the scene, attracted by the commotion.

The commotion also attracts one of the *agoranomoi*, an official charged with maintaining good order in the market. This man quiets the discussion by the simple expedient of having his attendants whack anyone who pipes up unasked. Since the attendants carry substantial staves, this ensures a degree of decorum while the Hebrews and the muleteers each state their claims to Thratta's person.

Finally, at the muleteer's suggestion, it is decided that a neutral person should adjudicate – that is, a woman who can preserve Thratta's modesty by inspecting her back in private and thereafter informing the *agoranomos* what she has discovered. Fortunately, the tent of a respected herbalist is right at hand and so, with a face as innocent as a babe's, a muleteer asks why they should not take the girl to this woman and have her resolve the matter once and for all. Somehow, the muleteers fail to mention Thratta's connection to the aforesaid herbalist, so the proposed solution is accepted.

As she walks toward the tent with a market attendant at each shoulder, Thratta feels both hopeful and terrified. When push comes to shove, will her teacher and mentor be prepared to lie to save her apprentice?

The Sprinter

The city of Hermione is situated on the Argolid peninsula, where the city's harbours are protected from storms sweeping in from the Cyclades by the twin islands of Hydrea and Aperopia. The city is ancient, and Homer in his epic poem the *Iliad* mentions men of Hermione joining in the Greek attack upon Troy.

Symilos the sprinter has seen the old city for himself, for though the promontory upon which old Hermione once stood is now abandoned, the ancient harbour is still in use. Some temples here are also still in use, as they have been for more than a thousand years. In fact, before they made landfall, Symilos joined some of his fellow travellers at the ship's rail to watch an impressive ceremony that was being held outside the temple of Poseidon. It is not Poseidon whom Symilos has come to honour, however, but Dionysus Melanaigis, the Wine God of the Black Goatskin. (Why a black goatskin Symilos established after discreet enquiries – apparently this represents a more martial aspect of the party god, who wears an aegis of black goatskin when he goes to war, as even Olympian gods have to do from time to time.)

The thing is that in the late spring there's a festival to Dionysus at Hermione that – like many Greek festivals – has a strong athletic component. Admittedly, at Hermione these events tend towards the aquatic, as might be expected of a city at the end of a peninsula, but amid the swimming competitions and the boat races there is also a two-*stade* race (just short of 400 metres, or 1,300 feet) at the old stadium and it is in this event that Symilos wishes to compete.

While Symilos' real strength is in the *stadion*, a race of half that distance, Symilos' trainer won't let him run that for a while yet. For the moment, he wants to get Symilos running the two-*stade* race as though it were a *stadion*, and then a month or two before the Olympic event the runner and his trainer will focus the extra strength and stamina that Symilos has gained into the shorter distance. This race, then, is part of the athlete's training, but that does not mean that he should not pick up a bit of extra prize money to cover his expenses and, by competing, honour the god while he is about it.

Anyway, the two-*stade* race is also an Olympic event and if Symilos is feeling chipper, he might enter himself for both the *stadion* and this longer event. After all, one Ageas of Argos was so energetic a character that when he won his event in the 113th Olympiad (in 328 BC), he ran the 100 kilometres (60 miles) home that same day to bring his city the good news in person.

With this in mind, Symilos has put himself forward to the organizers of the festival under the name of Koroibos of Rhodes. This is not exactly cheating, but many local festival organizers feel that having a big star name competing does not so much add prestige to an event as demoralize any lesser runners who might think of competing. So, while Symilos of Naples might be discouraged from participating, Koroibos of Rhodes is quite certainly unknown – though aficionados of the sport might smell a rat, for Koroibos (of Elis) was the first recorded runner to win the *stadion* at the Olympics. Furthermore, Leonidas of Rhodes – recently retired – is the runner whom everyone, including Symilos, wants to emulate. The incredible Leonidas is the only man who has won the *stadion* a dozen times and he was still winning Olympic events in his thirties. If Symilos must run under an assumed name, it will at least be a combination of two of the sport's great men.

So, for the first three days Symilos was exercising, practising his sprints and enjoying the festival, watching the crowds testing the famous stoa of Echo where any noise made at the one end is reflected back three times, and joining awed visitors to the sanctuary of Clymenus to gape at the huge chasm in the earth, which leads directly to the Underworld. (No one likes to refer to Hades directly, lest they attract that dread god's attention, so this sanctuary uses the name of 'Clymenus', which means 'well-known and dreaded' to avoid mentioning he-who-must-not-be-named directly. Nevertheless, so close is Hermione to the Underworld that its citizens don't bother putting a coin into the mouths of the dead since they are going to bypass the ferryman in any case.)

All this was great fun but now Symilos, or rather Koroibos of Rhodes, has arrived at the business end of his visit. It is mid-afternoon and, naked and oiled, the runner stands with his toes just behind the line graven in the stone of the starting block. There are two dozen runners competing so Symilos knows that he needs to get off to a flying start. Not only will there be considerable bumping and jostling as soon as the race begins but things will also get really congested at the stone pillar that marks the finish line for the one-*stadion* race and the turning point for this, the two-*stade* event.

Greek referees at sprint events take a dim view of false starts and already the runners have been called back twice because someone leapt off too early. These runners will probably run somewhat slower because, in each case, the officials handed out physical chastisement on the spot with their long, supple and very painful rods of office.

When the race does begin properly, Symilos positions himself just behind a young runner who has kicked off with a desperate sprint. Knowing that he does not have a chance of actually winning the event, this young competitor has opted instead to show off to friends and family by holding the lead briefly before collapsing into exhausted obscurity at the end of the race. Then, as his pacemaker begins to get winded, Symilos easily steps around his man and in the process smoothly rounds the pillar that marks the halfway point of the race.

This is the most dangerous part of the event, for Symilos is now going head-on into oncoming traffic and it takes some nifty footwork to get around a slavering runner who charges forward, blind to everyone about him. By now Symilos is in the main pack, dodging and weaving frantically. He almost makes it out of the crowd when one of the back runners changes course and charges directly at him. Symilos is so stunned by the blatant attack that he almost forgets to dodge and takes a jolting blow to the shoulder that sends him spinning.

ANCIENT ATHLETICS FESTIVALS

The premier event was, of course, the Olympic Games. After the Olympics, the next most venerable games were the Pythian Games at Delphi in honour of Apollo. Unlike the Olympics, art and music competitions were featured as well, and there were also some athletic events for women. The Nemean Games slotted neatly between the Olympic and Pythian Games, and the Ptolemies instituted games of their own, the Ptolemia, which they believed to be equal to the Olympics.

He recovers within a moment and prepares to sprint the final sixty or so paces to victory when he sees a truly astonishing sight – there is another runner, not only in front of him but some fifteen paces ahead and going like a racehorse. This is literally incredible – even at this early stage in his training Symilos knows he is faster than almost anyone in Greece apart from a few other elite athletes, and he knows by sight anyone capable of beating him. Since there were no other elite runners in the race, there is only one way that this runner could have got so far ahead – as the pack of runners converged with the leaders already around the post, this fellow had simply turned well short of the halfway marker and started running in the opposite direction.

It's so obviously cheating that Symilos waits for shouts of indignation from the watching crowd and an admonishing bellow from the judges. Instead, there are just the usual race-day exhortations and yells of excitement as the race approaches its climax. Driven by a mix of fury and outrage, Symilos draws deeper than ever before and hurtles toward the finish line as swiftly as he has ever run in his life. With great satisfaction he feels the thin rope of the finish line touch his chest, knowing he has completed the event a quarter-pace ahead of his opponent.

He is brutally winded after the race and so it takes him a few moments to realize that the cheers of the spectators are not for him but for his rival whom the judges, in blatant defiance of reality, have adjudicated to have finished with the narrowest of leads.

Symilos is about to storm to the judges' podium to demand a reckoning when his trainer takes him gently by the arm. He explains that the 'winner' of the race is none other than the son of the archon of Hermione, a young man with a bright future as a sprinter. Given the archon's political and social standing, not only is there no point in protesting the judges' decision, but doing so will also raise awkward questions as to why Symilos was running under an assumed name in the first place. Best to leave matters be and accept that whatever else has happened, Symilos has had a great conditioning sprint.

As his fury subsides, Symilos is forced to agree. Nevertheless, he insists on going to congratulate the victor in person – for should that young man actually get as far as the Olympics, Symilos wants him to recognize the man who is going to grind his cheating face into the dust.

8

ΨΥΔΡΕΥΣ ΔΥΣΚΟΛΙΕΣ

(May – Setbacks)

The Bride

A Greek wedding is a drawn-out affair, and there is no one moment when the couple (happy or otherwise) are formally pronounced as man and wife. Instead there's a process, with the pair starting to get married at the beginning and considered married at the end – which may be several months later.

That said, Apphia can now consider herself a bride, for the first steps toward marriage have been taken and she is now irrevocably committed – or rather she has been irrevocably committed, because all that has been required of her is complete passivity. Her father, as tradition dictates, did all the necessary committing on Apphia's behalf and, indeed, Apphia has yet to speak a single word to Kallipides, the man with whom she has just been contracted to spend the rest of her life.

Apphia was not even present at the *engye*, that crucial meeting where her father and her husband-to-be sat down in the presence of witnesses and agreed that Apphia would be formally transferred from the guardianship of her father to that of her husband at a future date. To make the transfer all the more certain, it was here that Apphia's father handed to Kallipides the dowry that she will be bringing to her new household, and the two men sealed the deal with a formal handshake.

This handshake and the presence of those who witnessed it are essential parts of a marriage contract, Apphia knows, for Greek cities have no formal register of births, marriages and deaths. If the legitimacy of the couple's marriage is ever called into question, it is these witnesses who will be called upon to testify that the *engye* did take place and a dowry was formally handed over. Certainly, there will be plenty who can later testify that they were guests at the wedding feast but, without a dowry and witnesses to its transfer, Apphia would still be considered as little more than a concubine.

For a respectable woman that in itself is horrible enough, but without a legitimate marriage, Apphia cannot bear legitimate children who would have a claim on her husband's inheritance. The *engye* is therefore very important for her security and while she completely trusts her father, Apphia can't help feeling slightly aggrieved that she was not even present to see that everything went properly. It's her future life on the line, after all.

That future life is now rushing towards Apphia at frightening speed. In the eyes of her peers, she is no longer

GREEK FAMILIES

The Greek family home was the *oikos* – the management of which, *oikos nomos*, gives us the modern word 'economics'. The home was the domain of the women of the family – sometimes ruled over by a widowed matriarch, but more commonly a wife. Generally, a household contained several generations, for few Greeks lived alone. Unlike the Roman home, where the word of the patriarch was – literally – law, Greek sons were under no legal obligation to obey their fathers. Fathers did have a powerful means of keeping rebellious sons under control, though, for it was entirely in a father's power to disinherit an unsatisfactory child.

a *parthenos* – an unattached maiden with the freedom associated with virgin goddesses, such as Hekate and Artemis. She is, or soon will be, a *nymphe*, a woman who has lost her maidenhood but has not yet made the final step into becoming a *gyne* – a woman with children. It never occurs to Apphia that all these steps are anything but inevitable. After all, is not motherhood required for a female to become a complete woman?

Everyone knows that, once a girl passes a certain age, sexual activity and motherhood are essential for her physical and mental health. And if a woman is biologically compelled to have sex and children, it is certainly best that she does so within the safe confines of a marriage – and the sooner the better. Indeed, one reason that the bridal veil is dyed with saffron is because saffron is a known cure for the menstrual problems from which the bride is probably already suffering on account of pre-marital abstinence. For a Greek girl, the question is not whether she should marry, but who she should marry and how quickly.

Well, for Apphia the 'who' has been sorted out. Now everyone has to buckle down and work out the 'how quickly' part because a Greek wedding involves not just the bride and groom but also their parents, their brothers, sisters, cousins and much of the local community. There is, for example, the question of the venue. In the usual way of things, after the wedding feast the guests and family proceed in a raucous procession from the bride's former home to the household of her new family, where she is welcomed by her mother-in-law. In this case, however, the groom is living in the same house as his bride and it seems a little pointless for the procession to leave the house, parade around the block and return to where they started. Therefore Apphia's father is trying to book the nearby sanctuary of Ouranos as the venue for the wedding party. This would be useful because the sanctuary has a garden of suitable size and during the preparations Apphia can make her traditional obeisances to Ouranos Protogenos, as do all women wanting a healthy first-born child.

Kallipides is particularly keen that the ceremony take place during a full moon, as this increases the chances of the bride falling pregnant immediately, and the anxious groom has made it plain that the way to her formidable mother-in-law's heart is through Apphia's womb. Which leads to another timing issue – apparently back in Elis, the home farm is fighting fungal infections in the chickpeas and insect infestations in the main crop, so while Iphita is desperately keen to be present when her son finally is married off, she also has a farmer's pride in bringing home a healthy harvest. (Apphia has a gloomy premonition that within the next twelve months she will be able to converse fluently on the perils of diptera infestations in a summer crop and whether emmer or durum wheat is more resistant to the accursed bugs.)

The struggles with the coming harvest have required the dispatch and reception of several highly expensive messengers and now it is agreed that Iphita will head for Athens as soon as the crop is safely in and that the wedding will take place on the first full moon following her arrival. When Apphia complained about the difficulties involved in splitting her life between Athens and Elis, one of her sisters pointed out an important advantage of not being an Athenian.

Their father has no son and, were he an Athenian, the youngest daughter would be forced to become an *epikleros* – a vessel for keeping property within the family. On her father's death, said unfortunate daughter would have been compelled to divorce her current husband and marry her father's closest male relative, thus ensuring the safe transfer of the father's inherited assets to another male family member. Fortunately, Apphia's family are metics – resident aliens – and, as such, no one cares what happens to their inheritance, least of all the authorities in faraway Elis. Apphia has several uncles and the thought of marrying any of them makes Kallipides look like the catch of the decade, so Apphia is forced into reluctant agreement with her sister.

Apphia's mother is also frantically busy – she has to organize a purple wedding dress and hire a *nymphokomos*, a professional bride decorator who will ensure that Apphia looks her very best on her wedding day. Then she must schedule prayers and formal sacrifices – called *proteleia* – to what looks like an entire pantheon of wedding-related deities – not just Ouranos but also Artemis (whose divine custody Apphia is leaving), Hera (who takes charge of Apphia, both as guardian of married women and patron goddess of Elis), Athena (the top local god, who requires a further sacrifice as Athena Ourania, a fertility goddess), Hekate (a sort of celestial bouncer who will keep evil

WEDDING CEREMONY SCENE – THE BRIDE HAS HER FEET WASHED

influences away from the ceremony), Gaia (the mother-goddess) and Hippolytos (a demi-god devotee of Artemis to whom girls dedicate locks of their hair while yet maidens). Consider just the vases: Apphia's mother must procure the *loutrophoros*, which carries sacred water for the wedding bath, the *lebetes gamikoi* for sprinkling water over the bride before some of the ceremonies, *pyxis* vases on which a painter captures the wedding scene, and *alabastra* pots for the wedding unguents. Meanwhile, Apphia has had to get weaving – literally, because on her wedding morning she needs to present her husband with a garment called a *chlanis*, a light tunic that demonstrates her competence at the loom where she now spends most of her mornings.

She also needs to pick some recipes for the dinner she will serve her new husband's family on the day after her marriage – this dinner being the final confirmation that she is now an accepted member of her new household. Fortunately, in Apphia's case this will be just dinner for three and Kallipides has already informed Apphia via her father that Iphita will eat almost anything, though it might be tactless to serve her chickpeas.

The Builder

Meton the builder is a fan of the Doric order of architecture. He likes the clean, straight lines and the uncluttered functionality of a style devoid of the ornate flourishes of the Corinthian or the fussy ornamentation of the Ionic. And when one is looking at the basic architecture of a temple, nothing defines its architectural order more emphatically than the columns.

Consider, as Meton often does, column capitals. This is the bit at the top of the pillar, just below whatever the column is supporting. A Doric capital simply widens out until it is the width of its abacus – the flat slab of the capital's upper part – which actually takes the weight of whatever is above. Basically, the capital does the job it is supposed to, straightforwardly holding things up without making a production about it.

Now, if you want a production, go the full Corinthian, where the basic stone slab of the abacus becomes an over-engraved piece of complex moulding with its own form of echinus (don't ask) and delicately carved acanthus leaves on the main capital that take a specialist stonemason months to get right – and even then a careless stroke of the chisel can bring the whole work to naught. (Though Meton is not the only builder who has managed some crafty repairs to a damaged capital with marble dust and concrete. The repairs fall away in time, but if they have masked the mistake skilfully enough, the builder and stonemason are safely dead by the time that happens.)

One would think that the Ionic order might work as a compromise between the Spartan lines of the Doric and the florid exuberance of the Corinthian but, if anything, Meton hates the finicky curly bits at the top of an Ionic column even more. (Technically, these 'curly bits' are called 'volutes', though Meton prefers a somewhat more profane term.) His dislike is because the obvolute carvings beneath and on the sides of the Ionic abacus are both tiny and difficult, and in any case require a ladder for the true aficionado to inspect them properly.

The Greeks call the Doric order 'masculine' and the Ionic 'feminine', and it is masculine strength that makes Doric the choice for ground-floor architectural designs in a multistorey building, with the Ionic on the second level and, if needed, the Corinthian goes at the top where it won't embarrass anybody.

Actually, the 'masculine strength' of a Doric column is not merely a metaphor. Doric columns are indeed sturdier because the height-to-diameter ratio is lower than for the more graceful (and accordingly, more fragile) Ionic columns, while Corinthian columns are so slender that Meton swears he would not trust them to bear their own weight in a strong wind. A Doric column is a sensible affair, wider at the bottom than at the top because the bottom bears the most strain as it has to support the weight of the rest of the pillar as well as whatever the column is holding up. A straight-edged Corinthian column naturally sacrifices function for form and soars upward as though made of adamite, impervious to the stresses of normal materials.

It may well be that the most famous of all Doric-style temples, the Parthenon in Athens, is Doric precisely because the Parthenon is a massive building and the justifiably proud Athenians of those days wanted their temple to remain standing for future generations to admire. After all, some of the lesser buildings on the Athenian Acropolis, such as the Erechtheum, sport Ionic columns, but then they are not designed to carry several tons of marble in a manner that almost makes them appear to be floating on the air.

So now Meton stands at the base of the stairway leading up to the *naos,* the temple's central building, which will hold the sacred statue of Serapis. The *naos* has gone up well, for it is basically a straightforward box structure of solid stone blocks. The earthquake that threw this structure down did not much damage the blocks, though Meton was disgusted to find that some of the upper ones were actually thin sandstone slabs in-filled with rubble as a cost-cutting measure. His temple, funded by the wealth of Egypt, will be pure sandstone all the way, with bright-painted stucco facing and a portico of twelve marble columns in his beloved Doric style. Already the scaffolding is in place and cranes stand ready to lift the weighty column drums into place.

Yet the cranes currently stand idle thanks to an intervention from 'the highest levels' of the Egyptian government. Despite Meton's earnest desire for the Egyptians to give him the money and then stand back to let him do the work, King Ptolemy's agents seem determined to second-guess the builder's every move. As of yesterday, the erection of the columns has been delayed because it is apparently essential that they be fluted.

'Fluting' is a very common form of decoration for the main part of a temple column. Fluting might be defined as vertical deep grooves carved into the column pillar trunk (so long as one ignores some of the more outré efforts of avant-garde architects in such places as Syria, who are experimenting with designs like spiral grooves). Fluting is more common on Ionic and Corinthian columns and in

Meton's highly biased opinion, putting fluting on a Doric column blasphemes against the entire Doric philosophy of clean and functional architecture. The only point of fluting is to make a column look rounder, taller and slimmer – in short, it needs a lot of extra cosmetic work for no practical purpose. Nevertheless, the Egyptians have insisted and now Meton must reassign for the task stonemasons he desperately needs elsewhere.

Only later does it occur to the hard-headed builder that the columns need to be fluted because Egypt's Macedonian rulers are desperate to appear to the Greeks as Greek rather than as Egyptian. (While in Egypt's heartlands the Ptolemies go to the other extreme and try just as desperately to appear to their Egyptian subjects as more Egyptian than the Egyptians.) Enough Greeks have travelled to Egypt for it to be relatively common knowledge that the Egyptians don't flute their temple columns, which are in any case much rounder and tubbier affairs. So, from the Ptolemaic point of view, it is bad enough that Meton is using Doric columns, which are as round and tubby as Greek columns are allowed to get, but he was also planning to use them unfluted – Egyptian-style.

So fluted and Greekified the temple columns must be, though of course the original Olympic deadline still stands. In response to Meton's passionate pleas, extra money has been allocated for more workers to make up for lost time, though the necessary stonemasons remain so rare that Meton has seriously considered sending a raiding party to Corinth to kidnap a few. That the columns that are to be fluted are Doric is at least some consolation, for

Doric ones require only twenty vertical grooves around each while Corinthian columns (naturally) demand an excessive twenty-four.

Another advantage is that Meton can use the fluting of his columns to somewhat mitigate the dumpy effects of their slightly thicker bases. Using a carefully calculated formula, Meton's stonemasons will cut the grooves deeply into the column base and then gradually make each groove more and more shallow until they are mere dents when they reach the capital at the top. When seen from below – as columns usually are – the optical illusion this produces (called *entasis*) makes the columns seem higher. Therefore the viewer perceives the upper parts of the column as being thinner as a normal effect of optics and not because the bases really are thicker.

A disadvantage of fluting is that it produces lots of thin edges on the column, which are easily chipped or otherwise damaged by casual impacts. Architects using Ionic or Corinthian columns can protect the edges by filling the fluting grooves to shoulder height with round cores known as 'cables'. Convention allows Doric columns no such protection, and that, so far as the vindictive Meton is concerned, serves the Egyptians damn well right.

The Merchant

Pergamum, the capital of the city-state of Pergamon, is a boom city, growing at a breakneck pace under its newly independent rulers, and what was once a minor town surrounding a hilltop fort has already become a centre of Hellenistic culture equal to long-established rivals, such as Smyrna and Halicarnassus. For Sakion, still in the grip of his oppressive illness, 'boom town' might be considered all too appropriate a title for the cacophonous city of Pergamum, for there is constant hammering and banging as stonemasons and builders widen streets, throw up ever more elegant new houses and generally engage in the noisily creative chaos of construction. There seems little respite from the noise, which drives the already ill patient almost to distraction.

This is far from the first time that Sakion has felt that he was recovering only to be laid low once again by his fever. Each time he has tried to power through the debilitating symptoms knowing that his naturally strong constitution should be helping, but each time he has been forced once again to take to his sickbed and suffer through each episode. Doctors have been summoned and these have come up with a variety of diagnoses and proposed cures. One firmly believed that an evil spirit had taken up residence in Sakion's body as a result of his trip southward up the Nile and proposed a series of vile emetics to purge the body of 'black humours'.

Following the doctor's recommendation, Sakion now wears various sacred amulets, including one inscribed with the allegedly sacred Hebrew phrase 'Father, Blessed Spirit, the Word' (*'Abraucahdabar'* but which, following common practice, the physician has written as 'Abracadabra').

Most doctors feel that it was Sakion's ill-advised voyage

Magical spell against quartan fever

up the Nile that underlies his current illness, and perhaps the most credible of these was a doctor of the school of Hippocrates of Cos, who explained the matter thus: 'Water has a powerful effect upon health, and not only because it is best to drink water that is as pure as possible. One should avoid areas that are hot in summer, but which have large stagnant bodies of water, such as marshland. Such waters develop a strong smell and become discoloured, and those with such waters in their vicinity suffer from damage to the spleen, diarrhoea, pneumonia and mania.'

Sakion, pronounced the doctor, was suffering these effects as a result of exposure to the stagnant waters on either side of the Nile, and that exposure had taken the form of an illness known as quartan fever from its bad habit of recurring every four days. When Sakion peevishly asked how a man might suffer from merely having such waters nearby, when he had neither drunk the water nor bathed in it, the doctor had thoughtfully replied that the very latest medical theory postulated that such waters bred creatures too tiny to be seen by the naked eye. These creatures float in the air and enter the body through the mouth and nose, causing serious illness of the kind from which Sakion is suffering.

Even the historian Herodotus, writing 300 years previously, had known that the annual flooding of the Nile created swarms of insects, and he had reported that many natives slept on raised beds protected by fine-meshed fishing nets for protection from the maladies caused by standing water. When Sakion's nurse had protested that even fine-meshed netting can hardly keep out the 'invisible tiny creatures' that the doctor had mentioned earlier, the man had agreed, but argued that frequent infection and recovery had given the natives an immunity that Sakion lacked.

The good news, if it can be considered such, is that quartan fever is the most chronic but least fatal form of this type of disease, and if Sakion had been suffering from more vicious forms he would probably be dead already – instead of merely wishing he were. After two years, said the doctor cheerfully, the symptoms should abate and Sakion might end up feeling miserable only for a fortnight around the end of every summer.

Doctors have not been Sakion's only visitors, for a number of the city's leading merchants have called around, ostensibly to enquire about their visitor's health but also to mention in passing an interest in the goods that currently sit in a dockside warehouse awaiting their owner's recovery. Ill as Sakion may be, he has noticed that almost all the offers pitched for his wares are at around the same suspiciously low level and that while one merchant appears interested in his cargo of silk, another wants only the pepper and a third wants to buy his opium but nothing else. In short then, it would appear that the local wholesalers have stitched up the market between themselves and the division of Sakion's cargo was agreed upon even before it arrived.

To ascertain the truth of this theory, the merchant has taken himself to the agora on a day between the peaks of his fever. This is not an easy trip because the streets of Pergamum – as one must expect of a city which grew up about a mountain citadel – are steep and prone to hairpin bends, so that one must traverse several hundred paces laterally in order to reach a destination only a few dozen paces away but considerably further uphill. While this doubtless causes considerable inconvenience even to long-time residents of the city (many of whom seem to have developed splendid calf musculature), the advantage of placing a city on a hillside is that many houses have a magnificent view of the surrounding countryside over the roofs of those below. Furthermore, these hillside houses also benefit from winds sweeping in across the Mysian plain.

From the perspective of the struggling Sakion, it is fortunate that not every house enjoys these advantages, for Pergamon's hillside is not an uninterrupted climb. Rather, the city has three 'benches', areas of natural flat land where the merchant and his attendants can gather their strength and breath. Feeling his aching legs, Sakion reflects that legend may well be correct that the city was founded by

THE AGORA

The agora was the commercial core of a Greek city. Smaller cities had market days at regular intervals, whereas larger cities and maritime trading centres, such as Corinth and Athens, had their agora open on a daily basis. The agora was usually a lively, noisy and bustling place, which is why people who have a psychological dislike of such locations are said to have agoraphobia. Markets were far from an economic free-for-all. Most were strictly run, with punishments for merchants who sold faulty goods or gave short measure. Usually merchants purchased or rented a stall and the officials made sure that the traders were aware of the local rules – for instance, since wool was sold by weight, a stallholder could not sell a fleece that had been exposed to the rain.

the mythological Telephus, for only a son of the mighty Heracles would consider founding a city that requires such physical effort from its inhabitants merely to get around.

The upper agora, when one has reached the summit, is the main marketplace of Pergamum and there can be few places in the Hellenistic world where shoppers are more tempted to abandon the traders' stalls in favour of walking to the low wall surrounding the agora and simply admiring the view. It helps that the agora is on one side of the acropolis and so affords an unimpeded vista of the city and the plain beyond. That this may not always be so in the future is clearly indicated by the usual (for Pergamon) hammering and sawing going on next door where workmen are noisily constructing what will evidently become a magnificent altar of Zeus once building is complete.

A quiet conversation with the owners of some of the better-appointed stalls in Pergamum's market confirms what Sakion has already suspected. The price of the goods he has brought to Pergamon are as high as ever and the prices offered by the city's wholesalers are unnaturally low. This leaves Sakion with a choice – he can sail further up the coast to another city, such as Cyzicus, and peddle his wares there, or he can remain where he is and sell his wares piecemeal to the retail market. Indeed, several stallholders almost took his arm off in their haste to shake hands on the deals he offered. Another reason for remaining in Pergamon for the present is simply that Sakion does not feel well enough for further travels – and it will not be long before he has to return to Egypt and pick up the cargo of that accursed ivory, which he has promised to deliver to a temple in Greece. In the meantime, there's something else he wants to investigate.

In pursuit of their ambition to make the principal city of their kingdom into a capital of Hellenistic culture, Pergamon's rulers have begun to assemble a substantial library of classical works. This has aroused the jealousy of the Ptolemies who want no rivals to the even more magnificent library they are building in Alexandria and, as a result, they have sharply restricted the export of papyrus to Pergamon. Lacking papyrus on to which they can copy books of note, Pergamon's librarians have devised a unique new alternative made of finely stretched calfskin. This 'Pergamina' is more flexible and durable than papyrus and Sakion senses that the market for the stuff could be huge.

So, for the next few weeks, he intends to exchange his wares for as much of this precious vellum as he can obtain, and hopefully in the process beat the avaricious merchants of Pergamon at their own game.

The Lyre Player

Her tour through the Greek cities of Anatolia has been both pleasurable and profitable, but Kallia is now packing her things and preparing to move on. It is now time to leave Pergamum and return to mainland Greece. There are aspects of Syrian music that she wants to integrate into her own compositions, and also the haunting folk songs from Caria, tunes that the locals have assured her come from vanished peoples of over a thousand years ago. Ancient as these tunes might be to the Carians, they will seem fresh and new to the people of Achaea, which is the region of mainland Greece that Kallia calls home.

Also, in Greece the summer festival season is kicking into high gear and entertainers of all kinds are in demand both for public events and for the private parties that generally accompany the official celebrations. First, Kallia plans to hop across the Aegean Sea to the island of Euboea where she is reasonably sure of gainful employment at the late spring festival of the Artemisia in the city of Chalkis.

Almost all Greek festivals that feature athletics also feature musical competitions, which are usually referred to under the generic term of *mousikoi agones*. There are two types of competition, and while Kallia is as happy to praise the gods as the next singer, she tends to avoid *stephanites*, which are purely theological affairs where the best singer is rewarded with a symbolic wreath. Prestigious as that award might be, it does not pay for accommodation and it is totally inedible, so Kallia prefers to enter the *thematikoi* – contests where the rewards are in solid, countable drachmae.

In earlier eras, Kallia would have been able to find employment only at the private parties that run alongside the main festival, for by and large official events in the past limited competition to men only. Yet with the post-Alexander expansion of the Greek world to Asia and Egypt, the number of festivals staged by different cities has outrun the number of performers available to play at them. Consequently, city councils have been faced with the unenviable choice of either lowering the quality of the competitors at musical events or allowing women to compete. Generally, and grudgingly, the councils have gone for the latter option, though this is opposed by Greece's itinerant male musicians who have started to organize themselves into a guild (*koine*), all the better to exploit demand for their scarce services.

Kallia wryly notes that at the Artemisia on Euboea the contestants have to present themselves five days beforehand, during which time they will be fed and housed by the city. This apparent generosity is explained by the fact that the contestants will be required to provide the musical accompaniment to the processions, sacrifices and athletic events during the rest of the festival and be paid just one drachma a day for their efforts. (Music is a common background to track and field events – for example, few long jumpers or javelin throwers like to compete without a flautist or lyre player setting a pre-arranged rhythm for their exertions.) Still, Kallia will be passing the island of Euboea on her way to Athens so she may as well stop in at the festival, pick up some extra travelling money and enjoy the splendid roast lamb that Chalkis offers in abundance.

From there, Kallia will make her leisurely way to Athens, aiming to arrive in time for the Adonia, the rituals of mourning for Adonis, the short-lived consort of Aphrodite who died in a freak wild boar accident. At the Adonia, sexual discrimination is even more rigid than at other musical events in Greece but this time it works in Kallia's favour, for the Adonia is a festival celebrated only by women for women, and female musicians are eagerly sought for both public and private occasions. Thus well-paid employment at the Adonia is a given, with the only drawback being that the music accompanying the festival consists mostly of drawn-out dirges that Kallia finds wearisome.

That said, the Adonia might give occasion to get public feedback for a tune she has been working on, something using the Phrygian octave structures she had come across while in Asia Minor, but moderating them with fifths and thirds more suited to a Greek audience. Kallia is rather pleased with the piece and looks forward to playing it once she has found suitable words to accompany the music.

It is a matter of annoyance, not only to Kallia but to almost everyone in her profession that, while most athletic festivals have an artistic side, the most prestigious event of them all – the Olympics – does not. Consider, for example, the Pythian Games held at Delphi in honour of Apollo, where, as might be expected with a celebration honouring the patron god of the arts, a full repertoire of contests takes place. As well as sweaty men running and jumping around there are dramatic recitals, mimes and a full programme of musical competition, both purely instrumental and voice-and-instrument.

While there are no official musical competitions at the Olympics, however, unofficial fringe events abound. At this time, there are more noblemen and wealthy businessmen swarming the premises than are to be found together at almost any other time and place in the Hellenistic world, and these people are all busily trying to impress each other – and what better way to show off one's wealth and sophistication than by sponsoring a musical competition?

On a recent visit to the agora of Pergamum, Kallia's eye was caught by a notice for a particular contest, which is being advertised through all the major cities of Anatolia and presumably elsewhere in the Hellenistic world.

In order that all might celebrate the Olympic festival as finely as possible, King Antigonus of Macedon, through his envoy Persaeus of Citium, intends to accompany the festival with a musical competition to be staged after the conclusion of the first two days of athletic competition.

The first event will be the day after the procession of the athletes from Elis to Olympia, and will feature rhapsodes (poetry recitals), parodies (humorous take-offs of heroic poetry) and singing to the music of the flute.

The next day will be flute music and singers accompanying themselves on the kithara, *followed by duets and then solo instrumental pieces by* kithara *players. All contestants must be present at the conclusion of the contest to perform during the sacrifice which will be made to Zeus for the welfare of King Antigonus and the continued peace and prosperity of Hellas.*

What particularly strikes Kallia is the richness of the prizes offered. The category that interests her – singing while accompanying herself on the *kithara* – offers 1,000 drachmae to the winner, 700 drachmae for second place and 500 and 400 drachmae respectively to those coming third and fourth. This represents serious money, the sort of prizes offered to contestants at the great Hellenic festivals, such as the Panathenaia or the Ptolemeia, although if the contest is sponsored by the king of Macedon, Kallia supposes that the prize money can hardly be less.

Still, for that kind of money, a trip to Elis will be well worthwhile, and even though, as a woman, Kallia will not be able to watch the actual sporting events at the Olympics (where the men compete naked), she will at least get to listen to world-class music.

9

ΓΑΜΕΙΛΙΟΣ
ΟΛΟΚΛΗΡΩΣΗ
(June – Completion)

@@@@@@@@@@@@@@@@@@@@@@@@@@@@

The Farmer

Harvest time is when Iphita needs every man, woman, child and animal that she can round up and put to work. That's the end of the lazy days of late spring, of relaxed hours pottering around in the vineyard, lounging in shady seats in the yard and the easy decadence of sleeping until dawn. This is the month they call Θεριστής – 'the Harvester' – and no one will be getting much sleep until the month is over and the crop is in.

During the harvest, one aims to get a third of the work done before the sun is fully up, so Iphita always rises early. Even as the workers muster in the darkness, she has to make sure that they have their rations and tools, the oxen are yoked to their carts and everyone knows what portions of field they will be working. Harvesting begins as soon as it is light enough to see, while the stalks of the grain are still damp with dew and more easily cut. The cool of the morning makes work comfortable until the chariot of blazing Helios gets halfway up the sky and the heat scorches even the browned skin of the workers. Every day is a race against the sun – first to get work done before the heat becomes intolerable, and then at the end of the day to bring as much as possible of the harvest home before darkness falls.

Of course, Iphita's work began weeks before this when she took herself on personal visits to peasant households and local villages. Like every other farmer in the region, she is competing for the labour of these smallholders and for most of this month every rural village in Elis will be emptied of its population, with only infants and the very elderly remaining to care for the goats and chickens. Everyone else is needed in the fields and it is crucial that Iphita have long-standing bonds with the people of the villages from where she draws her harvesters.

Equally crucial are the negotiations with neighbouring farmers as to who can share which workers when. Fortunately, Iphita gambled on a winter wheat crop while most of her neighbours went for barley, a crop that is generally ready three weeks before the wheat needs to be brought in. This means that Iphita has a larger pool of workers to draw from, with the downside that many of them are already exhausted from a succession of sixteen-hour days – there's a good reason why bringing in a single harvest is compared to the stress of a five-day voyage across stormy seas.

To encourage the workers, Iphita herself is in the fields from before dawn until after dusk, urging the harvesters on and organizing them into teams that compete against each other as to which group can assemble the most shocks of grain in the shortest time. Once the prizes have been announced, the harvesters advance along the field in an uneven line, the men at the front. Each man grabs a handful of grain and severs the stalks with a single practised swipe. Then he throws this handful over his shoulder and even as he does so the man is stooping to seize the next bunch, while behind him a woman gathers up the stalks. When she has between ten and twelve handfuls, she twists a stalk of wheat around the middle and lays the assembled armload on the ground. Then her older children collect these bundles and bind them into stacks of four and leave the sheaves of grain standing upright so that the field eventually has little lines of sheaves for the wagons to collect and take to the barn.

It's a process that has been unchanged for at least a thousand years, back to when Homer wrote:

> *The harvesters mow the grain with swinging, whetted*
> *scythes,*
>
> *And as the stalks fall in swathes,*
>
> *The binders girdle them into sheaves,*
>
> *And stack the bands of straw.*
>
> *Behind them come the children, gleaning ...*

HOMER, *ILIAD* L.555

Not all the grain in the field will be taken, for custom dictates that one corner is the field's own share and that portion remains unharvested. Besides, the wheat crop has been substantial – insect attacks have been fought off and the ears of wheat are full and fat, so Iphita feels that she can afford to be generous. During the midday break, she moves among the little groups of workers who relax as they sprawl in the shade of the trees at the edge of the field, laughing, fooling around and gossiping. Because this is an occasion where folk from different villages meet and mingle, not a few unattached young men and women are eyeing one another appraisingly – and their parents are doing likewise as they measure up potential mates for their offspring.

Not for the first time, Iphita marvels at the energy of youth, for at the end of a day's gathering the only thing she wants to do when in bed is sleep, which she does very soundly.

Already the constellation of Orion has begun to peek over the horizon as the workers assemble before dawn, and this is a sign that the threshing of the grain will soon begin. This is hard and messy work – the piles of grain are laid on the threshing floor and labourers work in shifts to thrash the stalks with long, weighted flails. It takes several days before grain and stalks have been beaten into a soft mass, with fragments of stalk (chaff) mixed with the grain. Then winnowing can begin.

Iphita is keeping a weather-wise eye on the skies and has seen the feathery horsetails of cloud that signify a coming change in the weather. Should the strong, dry Etesian winds pick up early, the winnowing of the wheat will be done in a matter of hours. When it is time for this stage and the winds are right, some of the stronger workers will take their place outside the barn beside the piles of threshed wheat. They plunge their winnowing fans deep into the heaps and toss their load into the air. If the winds are light they toss higher, and in stronger breezes they aim lower and at an angle. Done exactly right, the grain falls at their feet while the lighter chaff floats off in the wind to be raked up and spread back on the fields to decompose. What remains by the barn is the yield from months of hard labour on the farm – pyramidal heaps of grain, ready for sieving and storing.

Once she has brought the harvest home, it will be time to gather workers and friends for a rousing party and send-off. This will probably last a day and a half, and then – after carefully instructing her foreman on what needs to be done on the farm – a somewhat hungover Iphita will hasten to the port of Pheia, there to take ship to Athens for her son's wedding.

The Diplomat

Despite his years of experience as an international diplomat, this is the first time that Persaeus has been in Alexandria. In a way it is surprising that he has not been here before, because despite all their rivalry, wars and jockeying for power, the Hellenistic kings like to keep in close contact with one another. There is a constant flow of ambassadors between national capitals conveying congratulations on the birth of a royal child, attempting to defuse a potential border conflict, or – very frequently – discussing a clandestine alliance between two of the great powers in order to discombobulate the third.

In the case of Persaeus, King Antigonus has decided to send his personal envoy to Egypt for several reasons. The first of these is that reports have reached Macedon that Ptolemy II is unwell and might be coming to the end of his long reign. Antigonus wants to know if this is the case and, if the Egyptian king is indeed not much longer for this world, then it is vital that Persaeus get a read of Ptolemy's designated successor, who naturally enough will be King Ptolemy III. (While Ptolemy II is a major irritant and a general threat to peace and stability in the eastern Mediterranean, no one denies that he is also a highly capable ruler whose succession has been as tidily arranged as all other matters in the Ptolemaic kingdom.)

The second reason for the diplomatic visit is one that Persaeus will energetically deny if anyone were so undiplomatic as to put the matter to him directly. Fundamentally, Macedon wants a war between the Egyptians and the Seleucid kingdom, because having those two rival states fighting it out with each other leaves Antigonus of Macedon free to get on with his own agenda. So it is the job of Persaeus to inform the Ptolemies (without ever actually putting it in so many words) that if the Egyptians want to go and beat up the Seleucids, Macedon will not interfere.

In exchange for this benevolent neutrality, the

Macedonians want a commitment from the Egyptians that they will stop interfering in Greece, and particularly that they will no longer give clandestine support to the Spartans and encouragement to that young nationalist firebrand Aratus of Sikyon, who seems intent in pulling all of the northern Peloponnese into an anti-Macedonian alliance.

Twisting Ptolemy's arm is going to be less easy than it seemed on the voyage to Alexandria. Persaeus knows full well the wealth and power of Ptolemaic Egypt, but it is one thing to know of something in the abstract and another to see the reality all around. In fact, Persaeus was impressed by Alexandria even before he saw the city. Their ship was still several dozen miles from port when Persaeus' attention was drawn to a flashing light on the horizon as though someone had somehow managed to float a silver shield on the waves. The ship's captain assured the diplomat that the light was not only on the horizon, but beyond it – what Persaeus was seeing was the light reflected from a huge mirror atop the tallest manmade structure in the world – the great lighthouse at Pharos. In later years, the captain added, a fire will be lit at night that will extend the range of the lighthouse even further.

As their ship glided into Alexandria's Great Harbour, Persaeus had the chance to inspect the lighthouse at first hand. Scaffolding still surrounds much of the building and workmen swarm all over it as they apply the finishing touches, but the towering structure is largely complete, almost a *stade* in height, or the same height as forty single-storey buildings stacked one on top of the other. This mighty tower occupies much of the islet of Pharos on which it stands, though a long causeway now connects lighthouse and mainland.

Meanwhile, on the left-hand side of the harbour is the Lochios promontory with its palace buildings, groves and serried ranks of apartments rising up the gentle hillside, all laid out on a scale more extravagantly gigantic than anything Persaeus has ever seen. As a royal ambassador, Persaeus is allowed privileged access to the Antirhodos, the secluded harbour used only by the royal court of Egypt, which is a pity because the diplomat can hardly wait to get a closer look at the main harbour. This is packed with ships of all shapes and sizes, from odd-looking Arab coasters to hulking Phoenician merchantmen and the solid hulls of vessels of the Euxine merchant fleet. Much of Ptolemy's wealth comes from trade and, as he struggles to remain impassive in the face of all this industry, Persaeus can clearly see why this is so.

The diplomat does not mention it, but he is also looking forward with almost childlike anticipation to seeing his first camel. He had rather hoped that he would come across one of these in Seleucia, but by the time they reach the Mediterranean seaboard, most international traders from the east have shifted their loads onto mules. The Ptolemies, however, have adopted the camel as the best means of carrying goods from the Red Sea ports to Alexandria and imported hundreds of the beasts from their home in central Asia, and camels are now flourishing in their new North African environment.

Naturally, the reception committee that met Persaeus at the docks was interested in impressing the diplomat not only with the power and wealth of Egypt but also with the fact that he is now in the new centre of the Hellenistic world. To that end, once Persaeus had enjoyed a night of positively decadent luxury in his assigned quarters, he was taken on a tour of the city.

Persaeus noted that he was carefully steered toward the Greek area and his escorts seldom mentioned the Phoenicians, Nabateans, Arabs and Numidians who make up a substantial part of the city's population. It was harder to ignore the very populous Jewish quarter, though, as this is very close to the royal palace and Persaeus had to pass through this to reach the rest of the city. Yet even in the Jewish area the native Egyptian influence is easily discernible, for while some official buildings have elegant Greek porticoes with slim, fluted Corinthian columns, others have rounded 'lotus-syle' columns of the native type.

Were Persaeus simply another eminent tourist, among his first visits in Alexandria would be to the tomb of the city's distinguished founder, Alexander the Great. That's certainly not going to happen here because, as far as the indignant Macedonians are concerned, the great conqueror's corpse is stolen property – seized from them on its way to a proper burial in Macedon and illegally interred on the foreign soil of Egypt. (The deed was done by the first Ptolemy as a huge propaganda coup, for the person who buries a Macedonian king is traditionally that king's successor. By taking and entombing the deceased Alexander, Ptolemy I was claiming to be sovereign of the whole Hellenistic world – a claim that his son and successor has vigorously pursued.)

THE GREAT LIBRARY

While it was probably the first Ptolemy who conceived the idea of a library that would house all the collective knowledge of mankind, it was his son Ptolemy II who brought the idea to fruition, though his successors built even further upon it until, at its peak, it might have held up to half a million scrolls. The library was part of a larger institution called the Museion, dedicated to bringing together the finest academics of the ancient world – and, as such, it arguably constituted the world's first university. Many of these scholars worked upon the texts in the library, and it is probable that what are now the modern versions of Homer, Hesiod and other ancient writers passed through their hands.

So instead of being shown this particular piece of Ptolemaic effrontery, Persaeus was escorted to the Paneium, a massive man-made hill beside the gymnasium (which is itself a hugely impressive complex of buildings) and from there shown a splendid vista of the entire city, already the largest in the known world. From the hill it can be seen how Alexandria is in the shape of a *chlamys* – a cavalryman's cloak – as it spreads over the large spit of land between the Mediterranean on the one side and Mareotis on the other (Mareotis being where the Nile has spread out to become a lake before this part of the delta reaches the sea). It is another sign of Ptolemy's careful forethought that

A DRAWING OF WHAT THE GREAT LIBRARY MIGHT
HAVE LOOKED LIKE

across the city are peculiar pits that will soon become huge underground cisterns, which will guarantee the city's water supply, come drought, siege or whatever.

Tomorrow, Persaeus will visit the huge complex of the Serapaeum and its Museion, including the famous Library, which can claim to be the world's first dedicated university. But already those giving the somewhat subdued diplomat the grand tour of the city have succeeded in their aim. Persaeus is well aware that Ptolemy's Egypt is too powerful and self-confident to be bullied or cowed by Macedon, Seleucia or even by both states acting together.

The Runaway

Thratta sits in her tiny room and contemplates a small linen bag filled with dried leaves, most of which are smaller and thinner than the last joint on her little finger. Her mentor Eudoxia had found the bag at a market in the small coastal town of Phokaia and had been extraordinarily excited by the discovery. So much so, in fact, that the pair had left the caravan and hastened north to Pergamon where the men who had sold the bag in Phokaia had mentioned that they planned to dispose of the rest of their stock.

What these men did not realize, Eudoxia had informed her apprentice, is that to the right person these ordinary-looking leaves are worth many times their weight in gold. Thratta more cynically wonders why the original sellers were unaware of this interesting detail. It is a sad fact that many of the cargoes that come down the Silk Road do not reach their destination in the hands of their legitimate owners. It is highly probable that the men hijacked the pack-camel carrying this particular load and were very disappointed that, instead of silk or spices, they had ended up with a sack full of odd-looking leaves that no one had the slightest idea what to do with.

Even though dried, the leaves are very aromatic and consequently this batch had been sold in Phokaia for its air-freshening scent. Because they are imported from the Far East, even experienced herbalists might seldom recognize the leaves for what they are: sweet wormwood, a very rare and precious plant. The thought that there is an entire cache of the stuff floating unrecognized around northern Anatolia had driven Eudoxia into a possessive frenzy, and once she had discovered that the cargo of leaves was headed for Pergamum, there was nothing for it but that she and Thratta had to leave for that city also – at high speed.

Furthermore, ever since that incident at Smyrna, relations between the herbalists and the rest of the caravan had soured somewhat. When the slavecatchers had grabbed Thratta, Eudoxia had extracted her apprentice from their clutches by not exactly lying, but certainly by bending the truth into something far from its original shape. She had, as asked, removed the girl's *peplum* and studied Thratta's back for an uncomfortably long time. Then Eudoxia had stepped from her tent and announced that she had not seen any trace whatsoever of whip marks on the girl's back and she was prepared to take an oath to that effect before any god and in any temple that the people of Smyrna wished.

Since the 'wanted' poster had clearly specified whip marks on the escaped slave's back, that settled the matter for most people. By the time that the slavecatchers stormed back to the tent with another woman who was prepared to offer a second opinion, it turned out that the girl in question had disappeared. Soon after, the caravan had left town, cutting short what might have been a more profitable visit lest the connection be discovered between the muleteers who suggested that Eudoxia check Thratta's back and Thratta's connection with the herbalist herself.

Although Eudoxia had been ready to swear that she

had seen no scars on Thratta's back, afterwards everybody in the mule train was very careful not to ask whether Eudoxia had not only removed Thratta's *peplum* but also her undershirt. There was a strong – and justified – suspicion that Eudoxia had not done so, and the caravaneers rightly came to the conclusion that they were harbouring an escaped slave in their midst.

This was awkward, because the caravaneers are a clannish bunch and Thratta had come to be considered one of their own. At the same time, local authorities everywhere are always looking for leverage that will help them to screw the maximum profit from traders and Thratta now constituted a major point of vulnerability. It was best that she went her own way as soon as possible, and the discovery of the little bag of dried leaves in Phokaia had provided the perfect means of doing this. So now Thratta is kicking her heels in a tiny rented room while Eudoxia scours the markets of Pergamum for more of the elusive wormwood – and also for the special type of customer who will pay whatever it takes to lay hands on the stuff.

The first day's expedition was unsuccessful, although Eudoxia did return with a basket of unhulled walnuts, which looked to Thratta's untrained eye like half-dried plums. Stripping the flesh from the nuts was a messy business, but Eudoxia instructed Thratta to keep the skins and juice. It turns out that walnut juice is about as close as the world has come to producing a colour-fast brown dye, and overnight Thratta has gone from striking strawberry blondeness to mousy-brown anonymity. All she needs now is some way to get the brown stain off her fingers, and then

MEDICINE IN GREECE

We know a lot about Greek medicine because doctors kept precise notes of symptoms, treatments and outcomes. This mattered because Greek medical care, though hair-raisingly primitive by modern standards, was still a lot better than that on offer over succeeding millennia, and the most effective medieval doctors tended to follow Greek practice closely. (Hippocrates' texts on amputations were still standard reading for battlefield surgeons in the First World War.) Even today the Staff of Aesculapius, god of medicine, with a snake entwined, is the symbol of medical care (though US practitioners through a historical aberration use the Caduceus of Apollo), and even modern doctors start their medical career by reciting the Hippocratic oath, with its famous injunction 'first do no harm'. Nevertheless, many ancient Greek doctors relied on a combination of folk remedies (sometimes no bad thing), superstition and religious mumbo jumbo, though again if the patient strongly believed in the latter it certainly did no harm. One Greek tombstone records the attempt of a doctor to cure a patient of a severely hunched back by placing progressively heavier stones upon his chest. It is uncertain whether the patient perished from a spinal fracture or suffocation, but his tombstone dryly records that he 'died straighter than a ruler'.

with a fringe of brown hair peeking out from the headscarf that also covers her neck, Thratta can again safely venture out into society and help her mentor to scour the markets for those elusive dried leaves. (Once hulled, the walnuts taste pretty good, too.)

This is more than can be said for the wormwood. As even an apprentice herbalist, Thratta is familiar with common wormwood, which is rubbed on the skin to repel small biting insects and taken internally as a cure for intestinal worms. As mugwort ale, wormwood is a useful cure for hangovers and Thratta has brewed more than several mugfulls for her mentor over the past few months. An experimental nibble of the rare wormwood proved so bitter that Thratta spent almost a minute trying to turn her face inside out. If that is 'sweet wormwood' she has no inclination to try the other kind.

That evening Eudoxia returns with news that she has located her customer for the wormwood before she has found the rest of the leaves. As darkness falls, she and Thratta travel uphill (Pergamum has basically two directions – uphill and downhill) to a well-appointed building with a splendid view of the Mysian plain. There the two are interviewed first by a young doctor and then by his patient – a middle-aged man whose near-skeletal appearance shows that his affliction is close to breaking him.

Thratta is no stranger to kitchens and when they go to prepare their potion it takes a while for Eudoxia to wrench Thratta's rapt attention from the room's variety of expensive pots and cooking implements and back to the matter at hand. Busy over her potion, Eudoxia explains that the man is suffering from quartan fever and nothing other than the leaves of sweet wormwood can bring relief. Carefully, the old woman instructs Thratta how to crush the leaves into the heated water, adding a pinch of willow bark to help with the muscle pains the patient is doubtless experiencing. The water must be warm enough for the essences to seep from the leaves but not too hot, lest the volatile oils boil away as steam. The buds that came in the fabric bag are not essential, Eudoxia adds, but they are included to demonstrate to the customer that the herb was harvested just as it was beginning to flower, when the drugs in the leaves are at their most potent.

Eudoxia explains that just this one jug of medicament that she and Thratta are about to take upstairs will pay more than a week's worth of normal sales in the agora, and once the merchant has experienced the relief that sweet wormwood can bring, he will be well prepared to keep paying for more. It is now essential that Eudoxia tracks down the rest of that cargo of wormwood, for she has plans as to how she can make a massive profit and, simultaneously, secure the well-being of that troublesome apprentice of whom she confesses that she has become inordinately fond.

The Sprinter

The festival season is good for Symilos the sprinter, who has spent the past few months travelling along the

Aegean coastline, partaking in festivals from Byzantium all the way down to Rhodes. Every city has its own cycle of events – some in honour of their patron god, some in honour of the founder and some in slavish flattery of whichever of the great Hellenistic kings either gave a benefaction to the city or had refrained from flattening it in the recent past.

All of these festivals have a religious component with processions and sacrifices, and most feature athletic and musical events as well. Symilos is usually welcomed at the athletic events, even though he has learned his lesson and now competes under his own name. Most of the sprinters against whom Symilos will race at the Olympics do their training in their home towns so the presence of an elite runner adds some prestige to the events in which he takes part.

When an athlete sends to Olympia notice of his intention to compete, he includes a guarantee that he will complete ten months of training before his event. Usually this is done in the athlete's home city where witnesses can certify, if necessary, that the competitor has stuck to his training regime. There are, however, always a few itinerant exceptions, such as Symilos, who can't even get to his home town because of the contingencies of war, and for these athletes, wins in local festivals allow them to produce evidence that they have been preparing for the Games all the while.

Indeed, it is exactly because travel is often interrupted by war that at this time the city of Elis sends ambassadors around Greece to announce the date of the commencement of the Olympic truce. After that point, visitors and athletes attending the Games are under the sacred protection of Zeus and the more practical protection of the Elean authorities, and they must be allowed to pass unhindered even through the lands of those states with which they are at war.

Those who might wonder how the relatively unmilitary Eleans are able to so enforce their will upon the rest of the Greek world (though not, to Symilos' regret, upon the warring Romans and Carthaginians) could ask the Spartans. Under the disingenuous pretence that they had not yet received the Elean herald announcing the truce, the Spartans once decided to attack the town of Lepraeum and were promptly banned from the Games, both as competitors and spectators. When the Spartans appealed their ban, they were allowed to compete after paying a fine of two *minae* for every soldier who had broken the truce. Since the Spartans had more than a thousand men participating in their raid, and one *mina* amounted to four months' wages per man, the Spartan treasury took a severe dent as a result of their king's rash actions.

It rather amuses Symilos that his trainer has recently taken to exercising alongside him and has taken up an even more severe diet than he forces on his trainee. Allegedly, this is so that Symilos has someone to compete with and to build a sense of solidarity. Despite such protestations, Symilos suspects another motive for his trainer's sudden commitment to diet and exercise.

They are currently on the isle of Lesbos, and about to take ship for Argos, after which they will travel overland to Elis and eventually from there to the stadium at Olympia.

All athletes competing in the Games have to report to the Olympic judges (the *Hellanodikai*) in Elis one month before the Games. From there, athletes are distributed to one of the three gymnasiums in the city and there they complete their training, with not just their own trainer in attendance but also another supervisory trainer who is allocated to them by the *Hellanodikai*.

During this period, not only will Symilos continue to exercise naked as he is wont to do in any case, but his trainer will likewise be obliged to deliver his instruction in the nude. As a top sprinter, Symilos is often the guest of high-ranking officials who like to show him off at symposia and his trainer generally gets to enjoy the same facilities – including their excellent cooking. Now the trainer is paying for his earlier excess as he tries to work off a stubborn little pot belly before he has to reveal his wobbly stomach to his fellow trainers and other athletes.

For this mortification, the trainer has to thank a woman named Kallipateira, daughter of an Olympic champion, sister-in-law of another and trainer of her son, who was also an Olympic champion. It's that latter qualification that almost got Kallipateira killed, because she insisted on going to Olympia with her son and continuing his training right up to the day of the event.

Now, on the way from the tiny town of Skillous to Olympia, before you cross the River Alpheus there is a large and very steep-sided rocky outcrop that the locals call Typaion. The Eleans have a law that any woman caught coming to the Olympic Games or even just crossing the Alpheios on a prohibited day will be taken to the top of the most precipitous of the rocks on Typaion and from there thrown to her death.

The Eleans have never actually put that law into effect but Kallipateira certainly tested their forbearance to the limit. Disguised as a man, she not only went to the Olympics and there trained her son but also then illegally watched the competition itself. When her son won, the delighted Kallipateira vaulted the fence that separated trainers from competitors, but sadly, while she made it over the fence, her tunic did not, and the resulting wardrobe malfunction revealed Kallipateira in all her feminine splendour. This was a major embarrassment and not just for the lady in question, because no one really wanted to sour the festivities of the Olympic Games by executing a champion's mother. In the end, it was decided that, as a member of a family of distinguished Olympic champions, Kallipateira would be let off with a stern warning. Just to make certain that no one would repeat her deception, it was ruled that thereafter all trainers who accompanied their charges to the Olympics should do their instructing in the nude so that no one could be in any doubt as to their sex.

So now Symilos' trainer huffs out his instructions as he gallops behind his far fleeter trainee, though Symilos has noted that despite enforcing abstinence on his trainee with the admonition that his conduct must be in harmony with the highest level of morality expected of a champion, the trainer has not abandoned his current liaison with a young curly-haired Milesian girl.

10

ΑΓΡΙΑΝΙΟΣ ΟΛΟΚΛΗΡΩΣΗ

(July – Completion)

The Bride

It is almost morning, and the last rays of the full moon light up one corner of the bedroom while a sleepy Apphia contemplates what have certainly been the most tumultuous twenty-four hours of her young life. Though some of the rituals of a formal marriage remain to be consummated, Apphia supposes that she must now consider herself a married woman – for certainly the marriage itself has been consummated. Apphia thinks back to her *proaulia* – a sort of bachelorette party – at which she had received meticulous and frequently bawdy instructions from her sisters about which bits go where; and now she grins at how much fun it has been putting theory into practice.

It helped a great deal that apparently no one had

bothered teaching Kallipides about the theory. So last night Apphia pretty much abandoned the role of the blushing bride and had taken the lead in demonstrating the practical aspects of the ribald wedding songs (*epithalamia*) with which the groom's friends had serenaded them through the bedroom door until the last of the choruses had been replaced with drunken snores. Yes, it had been quite a day – and night.

After the *proaulia*, the process of actually getting Apphia wedded had moved into high gear. Apphia's father had ceremonially cut tresses from the head of his daughter, a gesture that symbolized the cutting of her ties with her former life and the parental household. From there the bride was escorted to her *loutra*, the formal bath of purification, a ceremony Apphia found refreshing enough to clear the slight hangover caused by the illicit wine her oldest sister had smuggled into the *proaulia*.

By mid-afternoon at the lavishly decorated sanctuary of Ouranos, the men (including the blushing bridegroom) were getting into the swing of the wedding feast, with the family and close friends of the happy couple earlier treated to roast lamb from the sacrifice Apphia's father had performed for the success of the marriage.

The lamb, rather to everyone's surprise, had been imported from Elis, from whence it had accompanied the groom's mother all the way from the family farm. On arrival, Iphita had immediately closeted herself with Apphia's mother and promptly taken over the management and, to the family's secret relief, some of the expenses of the wedding ceremony. When Apphia's father had tentatively ventured a suggestion as to the playlist of the wedding songs that accompany every step of the drawn-out process, Iphita had sent him packing with a quote from the playwright Euripides: 'No, by Hera, the goddess-queen of Argos! Go and manage things outside the household but here indoors it is I who decides [what is proper for the bride].'

As the sun set, the matrons and girls joined the wedding party where Apphia sat, ensconced in her wedding finery and saffron veil, the subject of gentle affection from the married women and envious glances from the girls. Never in her life had Apphia been so much the centre of attention and it made her feel overwhelmed to the point of being giddy. She was somewhat uncertain of what was going on since no one seemed to feel that it was necessary that she either understood or particularly participated in events, but she was keenly aware of the moment when her new husband gently lifted the saffron veil through which she had until then been squinting at the party taking place around her. This rite of removal ($\alpha\nu\alpha\kappa\alpha\lambda\dot{\upsilon}\pi\tau\rho\alpha\iota\alpha$) was another of the steps in her transformation from bride to wife, as was the consumption soon thereafter of the sesame cake that constituted the couple's first meal together.

There was an immediate degree of empathy between Kallipides and Apphia, born of the fact that both felt they were being swept along by events controlled by others, an impression not greatly diminished by Iphita's constant stream of instructions for Kallipides relayed by his harassed groomsman and giggled suggestions from Apphia's sisters, some of which she was quite certain were not meant to be taken seriously.

Through it all, there was the heady smell of roasted food, the cacophony of loud conversations and shouts from the dancers, the smell of burning sacred herbs, the wail of pipes and the twanging of the lyre, all in a colourful swirl of clothing as flaring torches replaced the dying light of the sun.

At some point, Apphia became aware that the wedding party had somewhat thinned out and she correctly divined that several of those present – including her mother-in-law Iphita – had slipped away to prepare her new household for the reception of the bride. In this case, of course, the 'new household' would actually be the same building where Apphia has spent the whole of her life and where she will remain as a wedded woman for another month while Kallipides completes his studies. Then in August the pair will travel to Elis as a married couple.

At a nudge from a sister, who had been in close attendance, Apphia rose at just the right moment, keenly aware that the rest of the party had come to a standstill to witness this – the moment when they reached the entrance to the temple grounds and Apphia's father took her hand, pressed it into the (slightly trembling) grasp of Kallipides and then – having thus passed the role of male protector from father to husband – ceased to have a formal role in the proceedings.

Then the couple left the grounds while being bombarded with nuts, figs and dates by friends and family to board the ox-cart that would take them home to their marriage chamber. Again Apphia was the confused but happy centre of attention as the marriage party raucously

THE BRIDE TRAVELS TO HER NEW HOME

made its way through the streets, the young men dancing in circles, flutes wailing over the clamour of the lyres and those in households along the route shouting felicitations and congratulations from their doorways and upstairs windows.

As the party approached the garlanded doorway of the house where Iphita awaited with a torch held high in greeting, the musicians who until now had seemed more in competition than in harmony settled by common agreement on a single song that was taken up by the whole wedding party.

Deathless Aphrodite, Child of Zeus, weaver of subtle wiles,
Blessed lady I pray, crush not my heart with the pain of
    sorrow

But if once you heard my cry from afar and heeded me

Come now as then you came from your father's house

When you yoked your chariot, and the beauty of the swift
   sparrows

Drew you from the sky over the dark black earth.

[SAPPHO, *ODE TO APHRODITE* VERSES 1–3]

In the courtyard of Apphia's home, the celebrations had continued until the summer triangle of stars – the Eagle, the Swan and the Lyre – were bright and clear overhead. Then, escorted by her sisters, Apphia had tripped along decorously to her bridal chamber, there to await the moment when a gang of his friends seized the terrified Kallipides and tossed him within to join her.

Now, as she snuggles against her still-sleeping husband, Apphia is already looking forward to the wedding breakfast and to inspecting the presents that Iphita has brought her from Elis. Perhaps, she decides, married life is not going to be so bad after all.

The Builder

It is the fate of any builder that when construction is complete he feels a mixture of emotions – satisfaction if the job is well done and relief at having completed the project. Also, in the case of Meton, one might add bitter regret at the compromises made for the sake of speed, annoyance at changes forced upon his design by the client and mild embarrassment about the mistakes and flaws that, although invisible to the average visitor, are screamingly obvious to a trained eye.

There, for example, on the corner block – one can see that the alignment shifts a finger's width from left to right and a quick inspection would reveal a fracture running right through the block, carefully cemented though the break has been. This is not Meton's fault, because the block slipped from its harness as it was being lifted into place and came crashing down on to the stylobate, the floor on which the columns now stand. There were no replacement blocks available, so Meton had been forced to stick the thing back together and make the best of it.

The problem was that, in repurposing an old temple, Meton was forced to use second-hand blocks of stone. The providers of fresh material from the quarries offer dressed stone with knobs on the sides to which harness ropes can be attached all the more easily to hoist the blocks into place. Once set in position, the knobs are chiselled off and a wall of smooth, unfractured stone delights the eye of the beholder. Even the few new blocks of stone that Meton was able to commission are unsatisfactory, for they are perfectly rectangular, lacking the subtle curves and angles that can make a temple seem larger, straighter and more graceful.

The walls of the Parthenon in Athens, for example, lean subtly inwards, thus creating the illusion that the building is higher than it actually is. If the Parthenon were fifty *stades* high, the walls would actually touch, making a roof

THE FUNCTION OF GREEK TEMPLES

Perhaps the most important thing about a Greek temple is that it was not a church. A church is where a congregation gathers to worship their god and is designed to facilitate this worship. Anyone looking at the design of a Greek temple will immediately see that it is not designed for this function, and indeed the average worshipper did not set foot inside. The temple was literally the house of the god, and ordinary folk did not enter. The priests who served the god and did visit the temple were religious functionaries whose job it was to ensure that the proper sacrifices and festivals were performed at the right times and that the appropriate things were being sacrificed. Greek priests had no pastoral duties, and most were sublimely uninterested in the moral health of their 'congregation', most of whom worshipped other gods at other times. Ancient priests did not preach sermons, so there was no reason to attend the temple to listen to them.

redundant. Lack of time and skilled craftsmen cause the genuinely straight walls of Serapis' solid and hurriedly built temple to meet only at infinity, causing the building – in the resentful eye of its builder – to squat on the ridge like a deformed toad.

Meton conducts a quick mental inventory of the finished building from cellar to roof, establishing for himself what has worked and what did not, filing the conclusions in his mind for future reference – although, given the sum that his delighted clients have paid him, Meton only need ever work again if he feels like it, for he is now a wealthy man.

So, Meton is grudgingly satisfied with the foundation, which consists of the stereobate, the crepidoma and the stylobate. The best of the whole thing is the stereobate, which frustratingly is the bit no one will ever see because this is the underground foundation, built of beautifully squared-off granite blocks on a solid natural ridge of rock. No earthquake will fell the temple this time – the base is so solid that before a single column topples, Mount Kronos will have to turn somersaults. The crepidoma is three layers of stone, each slightly smaller than the one below so that the temple has three large steps all around leading to the stylobate, a polished marble floor only slightly crazed in the middle from having a block of dressed stone dropped upon it from a great height.

The overall design of the above-ground section is a neatly functional type called a tetrastyle amphiprostyle, with Doric columns (unfortunately fluted) fore and aft and a solid *naos* in the middle. The *naos* is the central chamber of the temple and it is built like a bank vault because that's exactly what it is.

At this moment, workmen are carrying through the solid brass doors of the temple, scaffolding and disassembled chunks of ivory that over the next ten days will be painstakingly refitted to make the chryselephantine [gold-and-ivory] statue of the god who will dominate the interior. The 'gold' part of the sculpture is a particular headache, as Meton meticulously has to account for every single speck of the stuff to his clients. Fortunately, what look like huge lumps of solid gold – such as the tumbling locks of godly hair – are in fact a tissue-thin layer beaten into shape over a wooden sculpture. Later, further offerings to the god will be stored in the temple cellar below – gold statuettes, votive tripods and other treasures, which every temple seems to accumulate as a rock gathers lichen.

Getting the statue together was another nightmare for the builder and one that had involved the dispatch of couriers right across the Mediterranean. Meton had eventually located the merchant who was meant to be supplying the ivory and had arranged for the sculptors to start work on the material even before the product was shipped from Alexandria to Greece. The gold had arrived separately in Elis and eventually Meton had shipped it back to Egypt so that woodworkers, sculptors and gold-workers could get their act together in one place. Eventually the merchant had shown up with the complete – albeit disassembled – statue and installation is now underway. The merchant's excuse that he was somewhat delayed by illness is certainly credible enough – the last time that Meton had seen someone looking that bad was a corpse being carried on a bier for cremation.

With less than three weeks to go before the Olympics, things are getting busy in the precinct and the first visitors are already wandering up the hill to gawp at the work in progress on the new temple. The stonemasons and labourers have mostly been paid off – it was a close race as to whether they or Meton's funds would finish first but

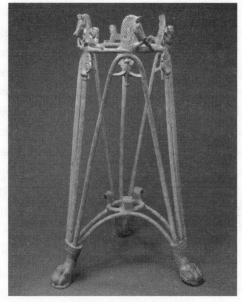

Bronze votive tripod

now that the Egyptians have paid up there's money to spare for the painters and sculptors adding the finishing touches.

A Greek temple is no monochrome edifice in pure white marble – the Greeks like their temples gaudy to the point of garishness. Column heads are painted green (with the paint made from malachite), the brown fake beams on the architrave are interspersed with panels of bright blue [azurite], while the floral decals on the wall are picked out in red [cinnabar] and yellow [arsenic] with the shadows artificially deepened with black from burned bone. The roof, of course, is flamboyant red with its clay tiles.

When the painters have finished, the temple will stand bright in its peacock glory, unsuited perhaps to the more subdued pastels of more northern climes but perfectly natural and normal under the glaring Mediterranean sun.

Meton studies the building for a few moments longer and shrugs. It looks beautiful, that he will acknowledge, but anyone who knows of the quick fixes and shortcuts involved in the construction would have to concede that this beauty is skin deep. Still, given the time and materials available, Meton reckons he has not done too bad a job.

@@@@@@@@@@@@@@@@@@@@@@@@@@@@@@

The Runaway

Thratta has returned to Greece, but not in the manner that she has so long dreaded, in chains as a recaptured slave awaiting punishment from her owners. Instead, she is a respected part of the retinue of a wealthy merchant and she is accepted as such.

It helps that Thratta no longer much resembles the slave described in the wanted posters she still hears being read out occasionally in marketplaces, for her appearance has changed greatly over the past year. Regular meals and a late growth spurt have combined to make her taller, rounder and more self-confident than the skinny runaway who fled to the Piraeus almost twelve months ago. She has been growing out her hair this whole time and, on those occasions where her neck is not covered by the wrappings of a modest headscarf, she leaves her hair entirely unbound, and her tattoo is now hidden by her tumbling and literally nut-brown locks.

She was sorry to leave her mentor Eudoxia behind in Pergamon and theirs was a tearful parting, not least because Eudoxia became highly inebriated and maudlin after celebrating her success at tracking down the remainder of the missing consignment of sweet wormwood.

With a business acumen of which the merchant would have grudgingly approved had he known of it, Eudoxia had purchased the wormwood from its unsuspecting owners at less than a tenth of its true value and two days later had resold it for twice its market value. The customer was of course the merchant himself, who was so euphoric at the relief that Eudoxia's potions had given him from quartan fever that he would probably have paid even more, given the unavailability of the drug from any other source.

At the same time, Eudoxia had considerably overstated the difficulties involved in preparing the tincture of sweet wormwood that had so relieved the merchant's symptoms. The preparation, the wily Eudoxia had insisted, could only be done by a skilled herbalist who needed to be in close attendance to supply the dose at irregular intervals. (Eudoxia had frankly admitted to Thratta that she had absolutely no idea what these intervals were and told her apprentice that she would have to work it out by trial and error. The good thing was that everyone else was even more in the dark than she, so any missteps were unlikely to be questioned.)

The problem was that his illness had already kept the merchant too long in Pergamon and he now urgently needed to travel first to Alexandria and then to Greece. In consequence, and in return for a further princely payment,

Eudoxia had been forced to relinquish to the merchant her apprentice, whose medicinal skills Eudoxia has considerably overstated. This separation Eudoxia claimed to have permitted partly because of her unremitting concern for the merchant's welfare but also because (she falsely added) her apprentice was almost fully trained and would soon be leaving her anyway.

One thing is certain – if Thratta had thought her training severe before the pair arrived in Pergamon, it was as nothing compared to the lessons of the next ten days as Eudoxia feverishly attempted to cram decades of herbal lore all at once into her pupil's spinning head. Item: the merchant is about to embark on a prolonged sea journey. If he or others in his retinue are afflicted with seasickness, what remedies are available? Answer: raw ginger from India alternated with doses of mint tea, because the mint tea helps settle the stomach, which anyway feels better for having something to throw up should vomiting become inevitable, while the ginger should subdue the nausea that causes the vomiting in the first place. And if rich meals cause indigestion, what then? Tincture of earth-apple, and so on for question after question.

So far, Thratta's precarious medical knowledge has not been seriously challenged, though her view of the world seems to need constant updating. When she was a girl, her Thracian village beside the river was all she knew and the mountains on the horizon marked the limits of the universe. Then came Athens, which contained more people than she had previously believed existed in the entire world. Then Halicarnassus came as a further

THE OLYMPIC CROWD

Every Greek city, town and village had its own calendar of festivals, whether these celebrated the start of the year, the end of the harvest, a significant anniversary or the deeds of a local hero or patron god. Festivals represented a chance to cut loose from the drudgery of a back-breaking agricultural existence and socially mingle. Over the centuries, some festivals grew in prominence, and these were attended not just by the locals but also by tourists who might travel hundreds of miles to attend. Not only did the festivals allow people to see the best athletes and musicians in the known world, but they also gave the aristocratic elite an opportunity to meet and discuss matters of mutual interest, such as trade and dynastic marriages. Everyone from Elis and Arcadia with a bit of time to spare after the harvest came to share in the general excitement, and every city had a claque of supporters come to cheer on a favourite son.

revelation, for no one had bothered to teach an illiterate slave girl any geography and the discovery that there were at least two cities the size of Athens came as something of a shock. Travelling with the mule train had considerably widened Thratta's mental horizons but nothing could have prepared her for Alexandria.

Sakion had taken a certain pride in showing his home

town to the wide-eyed Thracian girl whose gaze travelled incredulously from one wonder to the next. The merchant had also given Thratta a substantial sum of cash with which to stock up on herbs at Alexandria's markets, which were of a size and sophistication that left her reeling. She had even managed to replenish her sweet wormwood supply, though from a trader who had known exactly what he was selling and charged accordingly.

Now in Elis, it occurs to Thratta that she is actually more travelled than the average Greek, and by way of adding to her new-found worldliness she has persuaded one of the merchant's accountants to start teaching her to read. Progress so far is not great, but she can recite the alphabet from memory and by mouthing out the sounds letter by letter she can often work out the meaning of whole words. She has not seen Sakion the merchant much recently, for her patient has had his hands full with the delivery of a gold-and-ivory statue that is being installed in a nearby temple, and also with finding a venue to sell some of the goods he has brought from Alexandria specifically to sell at the Olympics.

While most people think of the Olympics as a major sporting event, it is also much more. Aristocrats and politicians from all over the Mediterranean attend the Games and, as a result, there is considerable opportunity for quiet diplomacy, the discussion of potential alliances – marital and otherwise – and of course the chance for merchants from all over to display their wares to discerning and well-heeled buyers.

It is precisely because people from all over the world

come to Elis for the Olympics that Thratta was delighted but not greatly surprised when her ear caught the sounds of her native Thracian tongue from a group of bright-cloaked barbarians as they exited a tavern. She established that the group were Thracians from the Macedonian border town of Akontisma who had come south to sell elaborate gold-worked brooches, cups and plates to those wanting to add a touch of exotic splendour to their dinner parties. Thratta was also enchanted to discover that among their goods was a small gold statuette of a horse that almost exactly matches the tattoo on her neck – a tattoo that for the first time in almost a decade has aroused respect and admiration rather than contempt.

Fortunately for Thratta, one of the Thracians was suffering from a skin rash easily treated with the judicious application of a compound of aloe vera and oatmeal. Though these Thracians are of the Satrae tribe and Thratta is of the Edones, the fact that they all are Thracians far from home has combined with Thratta's rudimentary medical skills to make her an accepted member of the group. She has been careful not to disclose the fact that she was enslaved in Athens, telling her countrymen only that her mother died while on a visit to Greece and she had since found employment as a herbalist.

The task that currently faces Thratta is that of training one of Sakion's servants to prepare the merchant's wormwood tincture because, when the Olympics are over, Thratta will be leaving with her new companions and going home to Thrace.

The Merchant

Sakion is encouraged by the improvement to his health afforded by regular drinks of sweet wormwood (which despite the name is appallingly bitter), and by now is resigned to feeling badly unwell at least once a week. Yet his appetite is recovering and he has considerably more energy than a month ago, when he could barely get out of bed.

This energy propelled him across the Aegean Sea from Pergamon to Alexandria and then to Elis, where he has delivered the materials for the statue of Serapis to a remarkably bad-tempered builder who at least had the foresight to start the construction of the statue before the materials had been officially released to him.

Now that he has discharged his duty to the Egyptian government, Sakion is free to look about for further chances for enrichment. Ever the opportunist, while in Egypt he took the chance to stock up on a few hundred sheets of papyrus, which were going cheap from a manufacturer who had overstocked, and he also still has some 'pergamina' for sale, the vellum writing material from Pergamon that looks to be even more durable and flexible than papyrus. For some reason papyrus only grows along the Nile (though apparently a single clump flourishes alongside the fountain of Ortygia in Syracuse) and therefore is in considerable demand by record-keepers everywhere. These scribes may even keep records of records, as is the case with the Olympic officials in Elis who generate mountains of paperwork over the course of the Games and who have already purchased almost half of Sakion's stock.

Consider for example, something as simple as a person's age. It makes a great difference if a lad is to compete in the men's or boy's events but how to tell if the athlete is as old or young as he claims? Many Greeks are pretty hazy about their exact age even when they are trying to be honest and upfront about it, because generally it really does not matter that much and there's a lot else going on.

Some states, especially Athens and Sparta, keep good records because age is related to military service and births are relevant to citizenship and so need to be recorded. But even then, Athens and Sparta maintain completely different calendars starting at different times of the year, and these as well as those of almost a hundred other cities and statelets have to be reconciled with the Elean official calendar. Then the name and presumed age of every competitor can be listed and the records published in case anyone wants to dispute them.

There are also the records of groundsmen hired for the event, workers who have been employed to dig temporary wells to supplement the waters of the river (because the river water will quickly become undrinkable after thousands of people use the banks as a bath and toilet), the roll of timekeepers and the judges' assistants, payments to caterers and a thousand other details that go into the organization of the Games. All of these expenditures and administrative details have to be meticulously recorded because the Eleans are very jealous of their custodianship of the Games and are determined that nowhere should there be the faintest hint of impropriety.

Normally, when several thousand people are going to be gathered in one place, Sakion would be looking for ways to make a profit off the crowd. But this is the Olympics, so he knows better than even to try – the locals had this all stitched up several centuries ago. For weeks, herds of cattle and goats have been gathered from the interior of Arcadia and are now awaiting their fate in the barns of nearby farms. Just as the animals have been gathered to feed the masses, so has the wood for the necessary cooking fires been gathered, stored and dried, soon to be sold by the bundle.

Already the first stalls are popping up outside the Olympic precinct, their location carefully predetermined by a shrewd local farmer who will also be renting campground sites for hundreds of tents, which will turn her field into a shanty town, with prime locations reserved for the pavilions of noblemen and wealthy merchants, such as Sakion himself. The stalls will sell everything from fast food to tawdry souvenirs to the services of fortune-tellers, herbalists and doctors of varied qualifications and abilities. Philosophers will take the chance to expound their views to the masses, and musicians will give the occasional free serenade in the hope of drumming up custom for later. Oh yes, and Sakion has heard that there will be athletic events over at the precinct, too, but he is not much interested in those.

What really interests Sakion are those pavilions of the wealthy and those of his fellow traders. For him, the

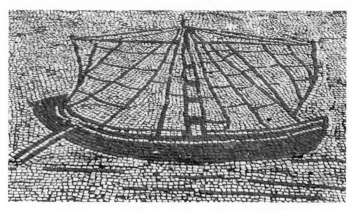

MERCHANT SHIP AS SEEN IN A PORT MOSAIC

occasion of the Olympics is a huge trade convention where he can meet with others in his profession and discover what goods are abundant and where demand is high for them. For example, the rivalry between the Antigonid king of Macedon and Ptolemy of Egypt has led to both kings jockeying for power in the Cyclades islands, and power there means sea power. Sakion will happily entertain any merchant from Pontus who is in the timber trade because Egypt is sadly lacking in forests and the government will pay any contractor handsomely who can supply ship-timber from the richly forested hills alongside the Black Sea.

It is a pity that the West is a financial disaster zone at the moment because the drawn-out war between Rome and Carthage has economically devastated both Italy and trade between the Levant and Carthage. There used to be a time when once could make a very tidy profit shipping luxury goods from the Far East to the tyrants of the fantastically rich cities of Sicily – especially Syracuse. Sadly, these days no one sane ships goods west of Corcyra (Corfu), since whatever escapes the hordes of pirates swarming the Adriatic is likely to be confiscated by Romans or Carthaginians. Thereafter the goods will end up being sold off by one or the other government as 'contraband' and the crews of the merchantmen will be pressed into navies desperate for skilled manpower.

When he has the time and energy, Sakion also wants to make his way to the sacred precinct, there to gape at the massive temple that holds the statue of Zeus at Olympia, one of the seven wonders of the world. Access to the statue in the interior of the temple is strictly limited – after all, great Zeus himself will probably be in attendance for the Olympics and who wants a stream of tourists coming through their house all day? Yet even the exterior is worth a look, for the temple is appropriately massive (70 × 30 metres, or 230 × 100 feet) and the exterior is decorated with statuary by some of the finest sculptors of the past two centuries.

Then at the temple of Hera nearby there's a masterpiece of a sculpture in Parian marble by the brilliant Praxiteles, where the great sculptor has created a statue of Hermes with the infant god Dionysus. It is only appropriate that, before he settles down to a week of intensive wheeling and dealing, Sakion should first visit the statue and there gain the favour of the god of traders and swindlers. After all, there will be a lot of trading and a lot of swindling going on very soon.

11

ΠΑΝΑΜΟΣ ΑΓΩΝ

(August – Struggle)

◙◙◙◙◙◙◙◙◙◙◙◙◙◙◙◙◙◙◙◙◙◙◙◙

The Sprinter (Part 1)

In the background, Symilos hears the bellow of a herald as he makes a public announcement. The nature of this proclamation is not particularly relevant because the important thing here is the manner in which it is made. For this is the opening event of the Olympic Games – the contest of heralds and trumpeters. It is necessary that this contest is the first to be held at the Games, because it will decide who receives the honour of announcing not only the timetable of all the other events but also whom the judges have declared the winners of each.

Although the contest of heralds and trumpeters is the opening event, the Games can be said to have started three days ago when the athletes, the judges, their retainers, the record-keepers and a host of hangers-on gathered in Elis to start one of the longest processions in the ancient world –

the 180-*stade* (32 kilometres, or 20 miles) walk to the sacred precinct at Olympia. The procession takes its time, for there is no point in anyone arriving exhausted and Symilos had rather enjoyed the two-day walk with crowds gathered in every hamlet and village along the way. Of course, there was also the huge cheering throng that swept down upon them as they reached Olympia itself, where the spectators were already gathered in their thousands.

The opening ceremony earlier today, on the other hand, was a somewhat tedious event, necessary though it was. The day started with the sacrifice of a wild boar in the precinct of the temple of Zeus. Then a long line of athletes formed, so that each could solemnly swear upon the remains of the victim that they had completed the necessary ten months of training, and that there was upon them no ritual pollution (such as murder or oath-breaking) that would prevent their participation in the Games.

Next came the tense matter of the sortition, when the gods take a direct hand in the way that matters will unfold over the next four days. This is when urns are produced and the competitors learn how their event will play out. In the wrestling and the brutal boxing event of the *pankration*, there is one potsherd for each competitor in the urn. Every pair of potsherds have the same letter, and the competitors draw the lots from the urn one by one so that those who have matching potsherds will fight in the opening rounds. There were gasps when two potential champions were drawn to square off against each other and murmurs of sympathy when a relatively frail-looking lad was drawn against a battle-hardened veteran twice his weight and age.

Then another urn was produced, this one with an archaic depiction of runners in a flat-out sprint. At the sight, the crowd fell silent and there was a general craning of necks as the spectators looked to see which sprinters would get which lane in this most prestigious of Olympic events. As a recognized favourite and winner of the sprint at the Ptolemeia in Egypt, Symilos was one of the last to draw.

The gods have decided to give Symilos an inside lane, which means he needs to discuss strategy with his trainer. The lanes indicate only the starting position, and as the race progresses there will inevitably be a degree of pushing and shoving as the athletes bunch up. The best way to beat this is to get out front early and stay there, so as soon as he decently can, Symilos heads to the stadium with his trainer to work on a fast start. An athlete wants to be quick, but not too quick out of the starting groove because anyone who launches into a false start gets punished with a whipping by the judges' assistant. This is not quite a disqualification but muscles recently striped by a whip tend to have sub-optimal performance for a while thereafter.

The sprint is the climax of the Games two days hence, so the good thing is that Symilos has a while yet to practise. The bad thing is that he has plenty of time for his nerves to get wound up tighter than a bowstring and restless nights await as he tries to calm his growing agitation and get some sleep despite the raucous celebrations going on outside.

Always one to hold a grudge, Symilos had looked to see whether that young man who had beaten him in the Games at Hermione a few months ago is among his competitors. Sadly that outstanding young cheat is not

THE OLYMPIC TIMETABLE

Day 1: Opening ceremony. The athletes take the Olympic oath before the statue of Zeus at the council house, and sacrifice to their gods. The contest of heralds and trumpeters determines who will announce events and victors.

Day 2: Athletes start the day with a procession from the sacred grove, and spectators settle down to watch the equestrian events. This is followed by the pentathlon (discus, long jump, javelin, running and wrestling).

Day 3: Sacrifices to Zeus and Pelops, one of the legendary heroes associated with the Games. This is followed by the boys' events, and many private parties afterwards.

Day 4: The double-*stadion* running event, the long-distance race, the race in full armour and the climactic *stadion* sprint. This is followed by the 'combat events' of boxing, wrestling and the *pankration*.

Day 5: The victors, wearing ribbons on their arms and carrying palm leaves, parade before the temple of Zeus to be given laurel wreaths cut with a golden sickle from a grove sacred to Zeus. This is followed by a final bout of feasting and partying.

there. His trainer informed him later that the judges at Elis had decided that the young man's performance was too poor for Olympic standards and he had been barred from competing. Nevertheless, Symilos hopes that his former rival is somewhere among the spectators where he can see how the event is run properly.

The Farmer

Poplar wood is useful stuff. The grey and green streaks in the grain render it no good for fine furniture but the wood is usually straight and knot-free, which means that it makes fine fence posts and planks, pillars to support the stable roof, boxes for transporting produce and cudgels for whacking Olympic guests who step out of line. Poplar being a light, soft-grained wood, blows from such cudgels do far less damage than those of heavier woods, such as olive, but nevertheless clearly convey the impression ('impression' here in the literal sense of a mark or indentation) that the person wielding the cudgel is less than pleased. Every four years, the workers on Iphita's farm get extremely proficient at using these cudgels.

Firstly, there is the matter of squatters. Iphita has allocated for rent spaces in the field beside the river, but it is remarkable how many attendees of the Olympic Games seem to think that they can help themselves to a patch of it simply because they have turned up. Those who have had the foresight to rent their tent space in advance are understandably indignant when they find that a bunch of self-entitled strangers have chosen to camp there instead. Fortunately, nothing explains property law quite as clearly as a cubit-and-a-half of dried wood in the hands of a muscular farmworker.

Given that the new temple of Serapis is a clearly visible landmark on the hill, it is also remarkable how many alleged pilgrims have managed to get 'lost' while traversing Iphita's farm and end up somehow crouching amid the hen houses, up trees in the orchards or accidentally stealing goats. Again, there is this peculiar idea among some folk that food at the Olympics should be free (and it actually is, given generous enough sponsors at the major banquets – but only on the final day). Therefore, those improvident wretches who have brought with them neither rations nor enough coin often decide to help themselves to whatever they can forage from Iphita's farm and livestock.

This is actually rather useful because one of the upper fields can get quite marshy without drainage ditches leading to the river. So far, there's a gang of fifteen amateur labourers digging that ditch for the price of three square meals a day and Iphita's promise not to tell the authorities in their home towns that they were caught thieving (reputation is very important to a Greek). There's still another two days of the Games to go and before then Iphita's workers and guard dogs can confidently be expected to add at least another half-dozen volunteers to their involuntary work crew.

Those hungry people who do have coin need merely tramp to the edge of the field to receive an excellent meal at only somewhat unreasonable prices. Many places in the impromptu Olympic village offer foods catering to every type of taste and cuisine, but only Iphita's stall has the advantage of being supplied fresh from a fully stocked and equipped farm kitchen.

Even before dawn, early risers can get a quick meal of fresh-baked barley bread cut into handy chunks for dipping in wine, which is how most Greeks like their breakfast. Those of a more decadent persuasion might prefer a wheat-flour pancake made with honey and sour cream and topped with more honey or goat's-milk cheese according to taste. To wash it down there's barley gruel, diluted goat's milk yogurt or clean water still cool from the well (not to be underestimated, for only the seriously

MARBLE RELIEF SHOWING A FAMILY MEAL

demented will drink from the river once several thousand sets of bowels have been emptied into it).

The midday meal aims to serve fast food, not only because at this time of the day folk are on the go from event to event, but also because long line-ups lose customers. So hardboiled eggs, figs (fresh or dried), apples (ditto), salted fish (imported at great expense and sold at even greater profit), and of course the staples of fresh-baked bread and olives go flying off the shelves almost as fast as relay teams from the kitchens can restock them.

At the end of the day, most festivalgoers like to wind down and cook for themselves, so throughout the afternoon the stall is busy selling arugula, carrots, cucumbers and even chickpeas – though the latter have had to be purchased wholesale from neighbours with un-infested fields. There are also cuts of lamb, mutton, beef and venison selected to appeal to every budget and taste, some already on metal spits (available on deposit) for roasting over open fires.

Usually, exposed sides of meat such as these would be swarming with flies, but they are somehow absent during the Olympics. The more credulous type of natural philosopher accounts for this by arguing that even flies are obligated to keep the Olympic truce, so at the start of the Games the annoying creatures swarm over the river and remain there for the duration. The more pragmatic Iphita reckons that the acrid fug from hundreds of cooking fires might go further towards explaining their absence, but so long as the flies are gone she does not really care about their motivation.

Dusk and after is party time and there are not a few nefarious deeds perpetrated among the tents of the temporary settlement, for thieves and muggers are just as fond of the Olympics as athletes and musicians. By and large, patrols of whip-bearing assistants to the judges keep wholesale disorder in check but their remit ends at the edge of Iphita's rented field. Occasionally, gangs of somewhat drunken young men decide to celebrate in the more open spaces of the orchards or the recently harvested wheat field, and they can get remarkably pugnacious when informed that they are trespassing. Most of these young men, however, are attending their first Games while Iphita's family have been at it for generations. It is truly remarkable how quickly a pack of slavering farm hounds can reduce even the most belligerent miscreants to penitent sobriety, and the few who do decide to take matters further end up ditch-digging once their wounds have been salved and bandaged.

Overall, for those on the farm the Games are off to a splendid start, no matter how events are playing out in the athletic arena. Iphita is particularly pleased with the performance of her new daughter-in-law, recruited from Elis for the occasion (during the harvest and the Games, it's all hands on deck). Sweaty and confused as the girl may be most of the time, she's nevertheless working like a trouper and actually seems to enjoy the organized chaos that is so different to her sheltered Athenian upbringing.

The Diplomat

Generally speaking, serious diplomacy happens in public. The movements of such senior diplomats as Persaeus are keenly observed by agents of the great Hellenistic powers whose kings like to know who is meeting whom and when. Clandestine negotiations are all very well in the preliminary stages but at some point someone with enough prestige to be credible has to stand up and speak in his king's name. When that happens, everyone knows about it, so Persaeus' meetings with Antiochus of Syria and Ptolemy of Egypt have been noted and agents of the great powers have already apprised their masters of the gist of what went on at those high-level diplomatic meetings.

This is where the Olympics come in – there are high-ranking officials and government servants who have come to the Games out of a legitimate interest in athletics, but there are many others present who are interested in discreet meetings that, being indistinguishable from polite social contact, will not be reflected on the diplomatic record. Few such opportunities arise and those that do are eagerly seized upon.

Consider, for example, the small but strategically located city of Sikyon in the northern Peloponnese. Recently, the government in Sikyon changed dramatically, going from a tyranny to a democracy as the result of an armed coup staged by a young exile called Aratus. This was something of a problem for Macedon because King Antigonus had been propping up the tyrant with money and diplomatic support. Therefore, by definition, the new government in Sikyon is anti-tyrant and anti-Macedonian.

The Macedonian grip on Greece is already threatened by the growing power of two leagues of Greek cities. To the south-west of Macedonia is the Aetolian League, a confederation of cities whose inhabitants already have an unfortunate predilection for brigandage and piracy. Now a new power has arisen in the northern Peloponnese where a number of cities have banded together into an alliance that has a distinctly anti-Macedonian flavour. Sikyon is flirting with the idea of joining this 'Achaean League', and Persaeus is determined to stop it if he can.

Now, it would damage Macedon's credibility with Greek autocrats if King Antigonus' envoys are seen dealing with someone who has so recently overthrown one of these rulers. Likewise, it would harm the reputation of the newly democratic government in Sikyon should their leader be spotted in talks with the power that had so recently sponsored their now-deposed oppressor. But if the leader of the government of Sikyon should happen to encounter a senior Macedonian diplomat at the Games – for example, at a musical competition sponsored by that diplomat – where was the harm in that?

As it happened, both the musical competition and the subsequent negotiations have both been unsatisfactory, leaving a somewhat embittered Persaeus wondering if it is worthwhile staying at Olympia any longer. His first mistake was to allow a Spartan judge to adjudicate the musical contest. This had seemed a good idea at the time because Macedon and Sparta have been on bad terms for almost a century now, so Persaeus had thought it would be a diplomatic gesture to show the Spartans some respect in a minor business where nothing serious was at stake.

The problem was that at the premier event of the contest – singing to the lyre – there was one clear winner. This was a woman who had composed a beautiful tune and played and sung it superbly. Yet the Spartan judge had disqualified her on some specious excuse, though in truth his reason was clearly because firstly she was a woman – and the highly conservative Spartans have strong views on women competing at such events – and secondly she was from a minor city of no political importance.

Instead the judge had awarded the prize to a male mediocrity from a Cretan city with which Sparta has close ties. So much, Persaeus reflects sourly, for the Spartan reputation for honesty and integrity – though, in truth, anyone who has followed Spartan policy for the past century should not be too surprised to see citizens of that state plummet well below their much-touted high standards of conduct.

Persaeus had high hopes of the outcome of his meeting with young Aratus, leader of Sikyon's democratic government, because both Aratus and Persaeus had something to offer each other. Aratus was far from the only person who had been forced to flee from the Sikyonian tyranny and once that tyrant was overthrown, literally hundreds of exiles had descended on the city eager to reclaim the houses and lands that once were theirs.

The problem was that these houses and lands were now

occupied by others, and not all were toadies to the late regime. Some had purchased the properties honestly and saw no reason why their legitimate deeds of sale should now be overturned simply because the government had changed. These people are influential folk, and if Aratus is to keep his grip on power it is essential that disputes between returning exiles and current property owners be sorted out to the satisfaction of both.

So what Macedon can offer Aratus is silver with which to buy back the houses of those exiles who insist on going back to their family estates and money to compensate those returning exiles who will take a cash settlement in exchange for what they have lost. Persaeus has twenty talents of silver available for Aratus but in exchange he wants a written commitment that Sikyon will not join the Achaean League in the northern Peloponnese.

Given the insecurity of the newly established government in Sikyon and the certainty of large-scale strife between the returning exiles and those who now held their property, Persaeus felt he had young Aratus over a barrel. A firebrand the young man might be, but surely he was realistic enough to realize that without Macedonian money the democratic government of Sikyon was doomed to fail before it was even properly established.

The meeting started out well enough, with both agreeing that the singer in the lyre event had been unfairly robbed of her prize. From there both Aratus and Persaeus had spent a few enjoyable minutes swapping tales of Spartan perfidy before the pair had settled down to serious negotiations.

Immediately Aratus had flatly stated that there was no way that Macedon was going to stop Sikyon from joining the Achaean League. Indeed, given his recent success as a leader against tyranny, Aratus fully expected to lead the League almost as soon as his city had joined it. Yet Aratus had no desire for an armed clash with Macedon (not just yet anyway) so he was prepared to settle for a position of hostile neutrality if Persaeus would please immediately hand over the cash that Aratus needed.

Persaeus indignantly refused, pointing out that Macedon would get almost nothing from the exchange apart from the potential goodwill of the people of Sikyon – and even that was doubtful given the intense and justified Sikyonian dislike of the recent tyrant and the Macedonians who had supported him. If Aratus felt that way, Persaeus had said firmly, then may he have good luck raising twenty talents from elsewhere. At this point, Aratus had smugly given the news that he had actually been given not twenty, but twenty-five talents already and the soothing balm of silver was even now settling civil unrest in Sikyon.

There's no need to guess where Aratus' unexpected donation has come from – without doubt this is Ptolemy intervening yet again. Only years of practice had allowed the frustrated Persaeus to remain calm and inscrutable, all the while mentally damning that interfering pharaoh to the darkest corners of Tartarus. When Persaeus had met Ptolemy in Alexandria, he had been assured that the Egyptians were done with meddling in Greek affairs. So much for Egyptian lies.

Well, the meeting with Aratus was a failure and the

musical competition an embarrassment. Now, sitting gloomily in his tent, Persaeus decides that all that remains of the Olympics is for him to take an interest in the actual Games. It's the climactic sprint event tomorrow, and with all other business concluded, he might as well take a front-row place and see how that turns out.

@@@@@@@@@@@@@@@@@@@@@@@@@@@@@@@

The Sprinter (Part 2)

And so, finally, the moment has arrived – the moment for which Symilos has been training for the greater part of his life. The feeling, he discovers, is rather similar to that of over-speed training, when the *gymnastes* has his athlete running fast down a steep slope so that his mind might become accustomed to his limbs moving at unnaturally rapid speeds. Part of Symilos can't wait to get out on to the track and there explode the nervous energy that has been building inside him for the past few days; yet another part of him does not want to go out there at all. This is what his entire life has been leading up to – when it is over, for better or worse, what remains for him to achieve?

Before the event, Symilos was at the gymnasium gently warming up under the worried and attentive eye of his trainer while spectators watching the athletes called advice and encouragement from behind the ropes that held them back. Then came the trumpet call summoning spectators and competitors alike to the main event of the Games.

Indeed, for almost a century this was not merely the main event but the only event – the *stadion* sprint, with the distance said to be determined by that which mighty Heracles could run with a single breath. Other contests have been added since, so now the Olympic stadium also features such events as the discus, the long jump and the pentathlon, yet it remains custom-built for the one race it was designed to host.

His trainer leaves Symilos at the start of the avenue of statues, down which the sprinter now walks with his fellow competitors, all of them naked, lightly oiled and gleaming with health. The statues beneath which they pass are a salutary warning, for all were constructed with the proceeds of fines levelled against athletes who cheated or in some other way broke the Olympic regulations.

Now they come to the roofed-over entrance called the 'hidden gate' and through this they see the *stadion* proper. This track has been in use for just over a century, replacing the ancient track somewhat further west, which was incapable of accommodating the tens of thousands of spectators who wanted to see the event. There are no seats at the *stadion*, other than those for the president of the Games and the judges, so everyone else stands on gently sloping earthen banks that rise to around three metres (ten feet) higher than the track, some 40,000 onlookers in all. There's the occasional woman in the crowd for, despite the general prohibition of female attendance, unmarried females are allowed to watch the sprint, and chief of all these women is the priestess of Demeter Chamyne, who sits on a throne of white marble opposite the judges.

Symilos sees little of this, for he and the small crowd of his fellow athletes are intent on making their way to the 'tomb of Endymion', beside which there is a line of marble slabs with a double groove indented into the stone. The elaborate starting gates such as one finds at the Ismithian games or at Delos are not for the rigidly traditional Olympics. Here one stands with toes dug into the first marble groove, keenly aware that stiff penalties await those who cross the groove of the second line before the start. At the end of the course, exactly 192 metres (600 feet) away, is a similar set of marble grooves – the winner will be the first to cross over these.

Another trumpet call, and Symilos steps up to his place near the middle, with seven runners to his left and twelve to his right. His entire attention now is on the track, a layer of clay smoothed perfectly flat with a thin coating of sand on top for traction. Symilos had been but vaguely aware of the roar of the gigantic crowd and he only really notices it when the entire mass of humanity falls silent and all eyes turn to the chief judge, who looks along the line of athletes and deems them ready. The judge nods to the herald, who takes a deep breath. *'Aaaaaa – pate!'*

At the plosive 'p' of *'apate'* ('go'), Symilos is off and running as if for his life, and in many ways he is. He sees no one ahead so he knows he got off to a good start, and he now concentrates on simply getting his legs moving as fast as humanly possible, eyes fixed on that distant finish line. Yet, as fast as he is moving, there is a pale body coming into his peripheral vision and Symilos forces himself to run even faster, but he can't outpace the runner at his shoulder, who inexorably draws ahead.

Half the race is over and Symilos is still behind, though he knows that he is running faster than he has ever done in his life. He can see the back of his opponent now and he knows that the race is between just the two of them. The problem is that there is no second prize in this race, only victory or the shame of defeat; it is the thought of that shame that makes Symilos force himself to go even faster, burning up reserves he did not know he had.

Level, he is coming level. His opponent must be blown, legs and wind giving out in those last frantic feet before the finish line. The pair cross the line almost side by side, but Symilos knows that as he threw himself forward in those last desperate strides he was marginally ahead. As he whoops for breath, he sees the anguished face of the other runner and knows that his opponent knows it too.

Now the other runners have also finished, some crowding around Symilos to congratulate him, others disdainfully standing alone as they await the judges' verdict. Hands on knees, Symilos tilts his head back and looks over to the ropes holding back the crowd and sees that his delighted trainer is going noisily berserk. Even before the herald bellows his name and the thousands of spectators take it up, it is slowly beginning to sink in. He has won – won the *stadion* sprint at Olympia – and now the next four years belong to him, the time of the Olympiad of Symilos of Neapolis.

12

ΑΠΕΛΛΑΙΟΣ ΕΠΙΛΟΓΟΣ

(September – Epilogue)

〰〰〰〰〰〰〰〰〰〰〰〰〰〰〰〰〰〰〰〰〰〰〰

The Lyre Player

The gods give, and the gods take away. Now Kallia sits at the stern of a well-appointed state trireme of Macedon and reflects that her life might now be very different were it not for a chance meeting under a temple portico while the rain poured down outside.

Kallia was in Elis, returning from a function in which she had serenaded a private party through a formal luncheon. She reflects somewhat bitterly that no one at that occasion had objected to her *kithara*, as no one had on any previous occasion. Yet that self-righteous prig of a Spartan judge had seen fit to disqualify her on the grounds that her lyre has ten strings rather than the traditional six. As if ten-string lyres have not been commonplace now for almost a century – and if having such a lyre were indeed grounds for disqualification, perhaps someone might have had the courtesy to mention this before Kallia had stepped up and sung her piece?

It was a good song, too – one that she has been working on since Pergamon, which incorporates a sense of the haunting Carian melody with a brisk Phrygian mini-cadenza in counterpoint to the rising iambic rhythm of the opening. For the rest, Kallia has mimicked the word accents of her song though transposing the opening high note and the lower note of the second line to give her tune an unexpected twist. The piece had been greeted with applause almost as enthusiastic as the crowd's booing of the judge who had unfairly disqualified her, but while she had certainly won a moral victory, Kallia had reflected bitterly that a professional musician can hardly live off morals.

Then had come that unexpected thunderstorm in Elis. Clutching her precious lyre in its leather case, Kallia had scuttled out of the rain under a temple portico to stand next to a stocky, bald individual who was glaring at the column pediments. Apparently there was something wrong with the abacus, or was it that the entablature was wrong for the type of pilaster? In any case, Kallia had shown polite interest while actually listening to the family drama taking place behind her.

A girl with curly blonde hair escaping from behind her veil was cuddled beneath her husband's cloak while aforesaid husband and a dumpy, grey-haired woman argued uninhibitedly. It seemed that the girl had just discovered that she was pregnant and her mother-in-law was insisting on taking her back to the family farm for the period of her pregnancy. The husband was arguing that

THE TEN-STRING LYRE WAS NOT POPULAR IN SPARTA

she should stay in the city but was clearly losing his case.

There was a stir as another group hurried in from the driving rain and Kallia noted with disdain that the principal figure of the group was none other than that diplomat from whose competition Kallia had been disqualified. The new arrival ordered a chair for himself from a temple attendant who had been lurking about the back, and as the man hurried to obey, Kallia saw that the diplomat's entourage now included that rangy young runner who was the hero of the hour, along with someone

253

who could only be his trainer, judging by the close attention he lavished on his charge. Symikolos? Kymilos? Anyway, he who had won the *stadion* sprint. Already the athlete had the slightly hunted look of one who has discovered that being hounded day and night by adoring fans is not all that it is cracked up to be.

Hardly had the diplomat settled on his chair when he was politely approached by a young woman with rich brown hair and a Thracian horse tattoo on her neck. The girl gestured to a gaunt-looking man had been sheltering with her under the portico, shivering despite his rich cloak, and after giving that man a long, thoughtful stare, the diplomat had given up his seat and, in doing so, for the first time had noticed Kallia.

Only years of dealing with aristocratic patrons prevented Kallia from suggesting exactly where Persaeus could stick his apologies for the outcome of the contest. Then, in a very undiplomatic manner, Persaeus had added insult to injury with an apparently offhand suggestion that she might consider a career as a musician at the Macedonian royal court.

It took almost a minute before Kallia realized that this was a genuine offer and not merely a humourless joke in bad taste. Persaeus had made his proposition so diffidently and indirectly that Kallia eventually grasped that the man was actually worried that she might turn him down. That is, turn down the kind of position that any musician would seriously consider selling her first-born child to obtain. Instead, her initially haughty reaction to his presumed 'joke' had caused the flustered diplomat to double a

THE SONG OF SEIKILOS

The song attributed here to the fictional Kallia is a real song from the Hellenistic era and is in fact the oldest song in the world complete with musical notation, so that it can be played and sung almost exactly as we have Kallia sing it at the Olympics in 248 BC. The piece was inscribed on a tombstone of one Seikilos, though it is uncertain if he or another was buried beneath it. The dedication is to 'Euterpe', the muse of music, and it is probable but not certain that Seikilos is the true author of the piece.

proposed stipend already considerably larger than sums Kallia had only previously met in her wildest dreams.

It turned out that Persaeus had tried to contact Kallia immediately after she had stormed out of the contest because of her disqualification, and until their fortuitous meeting under the temple portico he had resigned himself to leaving Greece without having secured the services of this talented songbird. Now he was as determined to hire Kallia as Kallia was determined not to let this once-in-a-lifetime opportunity slip through her hands. Consequently, through fear that the other would walk away, each had tiptoed on eggshells through the final negotiations, unaware that it would actually take heavy machinery to tear them apart.

Now, as she watches the ominous outline of

cloud-wreathed Mount Athos slowly slip below the horizon, Kallia stretches, cat-like, with satisfaction, and under her breath she quietly sings the song that soon will become commonplace across Greece.

Live! And while you live, shine.

Don't be troubled

By grief at all.

You live in the moment,

For a moment.

Then time will take

His due.

(THE ODE OF SEIKILOS TO EUTERPE, MUSE OF MUSIC)

@@@@@@@@@@@@@@@@@@@@@@@@@@@@

The Runaway

It is mid-morning, and where the hills begin to slope down to the river, a girl stands on a ridge that overlooks a valley. Below is the village, and it is just as she remembers it – the untidy jumble of houses with woodsmoke filtering through the thatch, the fields by the river bare after the harvest and the sheep like puffy clouds of wool. For a long time, she stands there silently, contemplating the sight that for so long was summed up in the single world – 'home'.

After a while, the girl speaks quietly to herself, as though working something out. She tells her younger self that there it is – home – the village seen only in dreams these past seven years. Those mountains on the horizon are exactly as they were, but Thratta had always thought old Ioxdel's house was somewhat closer to the river. She remembers how she used to play there, and his wife would come rushing out, afraid that she was going to fall into the water.

All she has to do is walk down this path, here, and in less than an hour Thratta will be surrounded by Thracian villagers crowding about, asking questions, some crying as they recognize her, returned after all these years as though from the dead.

Thratta sighs and shakes her head almost apologetically, for she is not going down to the village after all. It has been too long and though the village has not changed, the people in it have. Someone else now farms her father's fields, and look – it is clear someone else now occupies her old home. If she were to go down now, after that first welcome no one would know what to do with her, what to do with the lands that should be hers. Probably they'll sort it out by a marriage, as the elders so often do, and she will be paired off with a son or cousin of whoever owns her property now.

But that's not even the main reason she can't go down there. If she goes, they'll never let her leave, and Thratta is no longer that child who would have grown up there, content to marry, raise children, feed chickens and weave blankets from the rough wool of mountain sheep. She came here because that is what she had promised her younger self, and the knowledge that she would one day keep that promise is what had kept her going through those hard, hungry times in Athens. All those times when she lay sobbing on that thin blanket that passed for a bed, she had survived because she knew with certainty that one day she would stand on this ridge where she is standing now and see her home village spread out below with the river alongside and the mountains on the horizon.

But she can't go back. That village that was once her world would be a cage for her now, after the island cities of the Aegean Sea, the Lighthouse of Alexandria and the markets of Pergamon. Sakion will be waiting for her when she gets back and, once he is recovered, they'll see the ziggurat of Babylon, the red, rock-carved walls of Petra and camel trains coming in from the desert to Palmyra. For better or worse, Thratta is not the girl whom they kidnapped from this village so long ago, and no one would see in her now that skinny slave who escaped from Athens. The young woman who stands on the ridge is Thratta the herbalist, citizen of Alexandria and the world.

So she has come all the way here to keep the promise she made to her younger self all those years ago, to close off that chapter of her life. But now she must go on, not back. Thratta is not sure whether she is relieved and happy or tearful with regret, but she is certain of what she must do next. She turns her back on the village, leaving her nine-year-old self standing there on the ridge, and walks unafraid into her future.

Picture Credits

Page 20: Votive bust of Ptolemy II, 285-246 BC. Charles Edwin Wilbour Fund, 37.37E, Brooklyn Museum / Creative Commons-BY

Page 25: akg-images / Erich Lessing

Page 32: Terracotta Panathenaic prize amphora, attributed to the Euphiletos Painter, ca. 530 BC. Rogers Fund, 1914 / Metropolitan Museum of Art, New York

Page 35: akg-images / Hervé Champollion

Page 41: Decree relief with Athena, late fifth century BC. The Walters Art Museum, Baltimore / Creative Commons CC0

Page 52: Sepia Times / Universal Images Group via Getty Images

Page 57: Illustration from Trinkschalen und Gefässe des Königlichen Museums zu Berlin und anderer Sammlungen, Volume I, Eduard Gerhard, 1848

Page 63: PHGCOM / Wikimedia / Creative Commons CC BY-SA 3.0

Page 70: Granger / Shutterstock

Page 80: Familial scene in the gynaeceum. Red-figure Attic lebes gamikos after the manner of the Ariadne Painter, ca. 430 BC. National Archaeological Museum in Athens / Marsyas / Wikimedia / Creative Commons CC BY-SA 2.5

Page 87: duncan1890 / istockphoto

Page 94: Lyre player with Kithara (author's own photograph)

Page 101: irisphoto1 / Shutterstock

Page 110: Physician treating a patient. Red-figure Attic aryballos, ca. 480-470 BC. Peytel Donation, 1914, Louvre Museum, Paris. Photo Marie-Lan Nguyen / Wikimedia / Creative Commons CC BY 3.0

Page 116: Zzvet / Shutterstock

Page 124: Wedding preparation. Red-figure skyphoid pyxis, Adrano Group, Sicily, ca. 330-320 BC. Pushkin Museum, Moscow. Photo shakko / Wikimedia / Creative Commons BY-SA 3.0

Page 134: Merchant ship of the classical era (author's own photograph)

Page 138: Symposium scene. Red-figure Attic bell-krater, Nikias Painter, ca. 420 BC. National Archaeological Museum, Madrid. Photo Marie-Lan Nguyen / Wikimedia / Creative Commons CC BY 2.5

Page 146: DEA / G. Dagli Orti / De Agostini via Getty Images

Page 157: Nejdet Duzen / Shutterstock

Page 172: DEA Picture Library / De Agostini via Getty Images

Page 180: Magical amulet against illnesses, third century AD. Papyrology Collection, P. Mich. Inv. 6666, University of Michigan Library

Page 200: Science History Images / Alamy Stock Photo

Page 215: Terracotta lekythos, attributed to the Amasis Painter, ca. 550-530 BC. Purchase, Walter C. Baker Gift, 1956 / Metropolitan Museum of Art, New York

Page 221: Bronze rod tripod stand, early sixth century BC. Gift of Mr and Mrs Klaus G. Perls, 1997 / Metropolitan Museum of Art, New York

Page 231: Merchant ship as seen in a port mosaic (author's own photograph)

Page 239: DEA Picture Library / De Agostini via Getty Images

Page 253: Muse playing the lyre, Attic white-ground lekythos, Achilles Painter, ca. 440-430 BC. Staatliche Antikensammlungen, Munich. Bibi Saint-Pol / Wikimedia / Creative Commons CC0

Select Bibliography

Burford, A., 'The Builders of the Parthenon', *Greece & Rome*, 1963, Vol. 10, Supplement: Parthenos and Parthenon 1963, pp.23-35

Faulkner, N., *A Visitor's Guide to the Ancient Olympics*, Yale University Press, Illustrated edition 2012

Gabbert, J., 'Piracy in the Early Hellenistic Period: A Career open to Talents', *Greece & Rome*, Vol. 33, No. 2, October 1986 pp.157-63

McKenzie, J. et al. *The Architecture of Alexandria and Egypt*, c.300 BC to AD 700, Yale University Press 2007

Miller, S., *Ancient Greek Athletics*, Yale University Press 2004

Newton, C. & Popplewell Pullan, R., *A History of Discoveries at Halicarnassus, Cnidus and Branchidae*, Cambridge University Press 2011

Onno, M. van Nijf, O. & Williamson, C., 'Connecting the Greeks: Festival Networks in the Hellenistic World', Proceedings of Anchoring Innovation in Antiquity, 17-20 December 2015

Panagiotakopulu. E et al., 'Natural Insecticides and Insect Repellents in Antiquity: A Review of the Evidence', *Journal of Archaeological Science* 1995 22, 705-710

Pedanius Dioscorides of Anazarbus, *De materia medica*, translated and edited by Beck, L., Georg Olms Verlag, Third revised edition 2017

Retief, F. & Cilliers, L., 'Malaria in Graeco-Roman times', *Acta Classica* 2004, Vol. 47, pp. 127-137

Rotstein, A., 'Mousikoi Agones and the Conceptualization of Genre in Ancient Greece', *Classical Antiquity* Vol. 31, No. 1 April 2012, pp. 92-127

Vitruvius Pollio, *Ten Books on Architecture*, translated by Morgan, M., Dover Publications 1914

Index

A

Academy gymnasium, Athens 115
Achaean League 62, 243, 245–6
aconite 109
Acropolis, Athenian 86
Adonia festival 187
Adonis 187
Aegean Sea 27, 105
Aesculapius 204
Aetolian League 243
Africa 49–50
Ageas of Argos 162
agoranomoi 160
agora/markets 31, 66, 72–3, 80, 109, 158–9, 160, 182–4
alabastra 174
Alexander the Great 5, 18, 19, 20, 69, 89, 132, 198
Alexandria, Egypt 7, 18, 46, 89, 90, 194–200, 225–6
agalma statues 102
aloes 156
Alphaeus river 13, 15
amphorae 149
amputations 204
amurca 147–8
Anatolia 50, 53, 64, 69, 90, 105, 131, 133, 155, 185
andron 139–40
Ankyra 64
Anti-Taurus Mountains 131
Antigonus II of Macedon, King 62, 64–5, 104, 132, 153–5, 188–9, 195, 231, 242–3
Antikythera mechanism 9
Antioch 131

Antiochus II of Seleucia 19, 61, 62–4, 65–6, 103–7, 150–5, 242
  made god incarnate 103–4, 108
Antirhodos harbour 197
Aperopia 161
aphractes 135
Aphrodite 80
Apis bull 40
Apollo 51, 54, 55, 188, 204
Apollonopolis/Edfu 46
apotherapia 119–20
Aprhodite 187
aquatic athletic events 161–2
Aratus of Sikyon 62, 196, 242–3, 244–7
Arcadians 21
archers, Cretan 72
architects/*arkitekton* 129–30
Arcturus 99–100
Argos 133, 162, 213
Aristophanes 79
Aristotle 97
Aristoxenus 96
Armenia 64
Arsinoe port 46
Artemis 34–5, 169, 172
Artemisia festival, Euboea 186–7
Artemisia, Queen 69
artists/painters, temple 128, 129, 220–1
Asia Minor 47, 64, 65, 72, 76, 132
asochyta 149
Asoka, emperor 107–8
Assyrians 48
Athena 73, 172
  Ergane 39–40
  Ourania 172